Love's Journey®
ON MANITOULIN ISLAND

Moriah's STRONGHOLD

Love's Journey®
ON MANITOULIN ISLAND

Moriah's
STRONGHOLD

BY SERENA B. MILLER

LJ EMORY
PUBLISHING

To Steven

&

To all my Haweater friends on Manitoulin Island

The Lord is a stronghold for the oppressed,
a stronghold in times of trouble.

-Psalm 9:9 ESV

Chapter One

....

August, 1998
Manitoulin Island

Moriah's drive home from the ferry in the rain was mercifully short. As the windshield wipers kept time with her thudding heart, she managed to pull herself together long enough to get home without wrecking her truck. She was grateful that Katherine and Nicolas were still on their honeymoon. They would not see her go straight to Ben's cabin to try to comfort her. It would have been unbearable to talk to anyone right now.

She told herself she was merely doing her job, being a good caretaker, cleaning up after a departing guest, but she knew in her heart it was more than that. She wanted to breathe the same air he had breathed, run her hand over the desk where he had worked, touch the bed where he had lain.

The rain was supposed to stop soon. The crew was probably at the worksite right now waiting it out in the cottage and in their vehicles. It was her job to be there with them, but she didn't care enough to put forth the effort. She didn't care about anything right now. In fact, she looked back with wonder at the significance the lighthouse once had in her life. Nothing mattered to her now except the fact that Ben was gone.

She opened the door to his cabin and stepped into a heartbreaking silence and too much neatness. Ben had washed his few dishes and placed them in the drainer to dry. It would have been nice had he not done so. She would gladly have taken care of them for him. It would have given her something to do for him. She removed the few dry goods he had left behind; cereal and crackers, a few cans of fruit, and placed them in a box to carry back to the lodge.

She opened the refrigerator and stood for a long time, staring at a half empty jug of milk, some cheese, an apple, a couple of eggs, and then she closed the door, unable to make herself remove them.

Everything in the cabin he had touched or purchased suddenly seemed holy. It felt exactly like the days after her grandfather died, when she and Katherine had folded his clothes and packed away his life. Grief. Pure unadulterated grief coursed through her now exactly as it had back then.

But he isn't dead. He'll come back. He promised he would! If Ben makes a promise, he keeps it. Whether it's to me or to the Yahnowa, Ben always keeps his promise.

Annoyed with herself for grieving over a man who was very much alive and well, she wrenched open the refrigerator door, jerked the milk out and poured it down the sink. The apple got tossed in the trash along with the cheese and eggs before she could change her mind. She would have to harden her heart and fight this sadness if she were to continue to function.

The towels in the bathroom were still damp from Ben's shower. He had once told her that the thing he loved most about staying here was being able to take a shower whenever he wanted; a luxury he didn't have in the jungle. Again, trying to tough it out, she gathered up the towels and threw them into a laundry basket.

Then she went into his bedroom and lost every shred of resolve.

She had planned to strip the sheets and carry them to the lodge for laundering, but one look at his bed, unmade, as though he'd climbed straight out of it, and she came undone. Her fingers caressed the hollow in the pillow where his head had lain and smoothed the coverlet that had kept him warm only a short time earlier.

Giving in to a primal urge for comfort, she removed her wet shoes and carefully slipped beneath the sheets, breathing in the scent of his body left on them and nestling the side of her face into the indentation his head had made in the pillow.

It seemed like today had already lasted forever, but the clock on the wall told her it was barely noon. Ben would be in Toronto now. He was still on Canadian soil. Self-hatred coursed through her. She should be with *him* right now instead of lying in this bed alone, trying to draw comfort from his scent on a pillow.

Moriah curled into a fetal position to try to shield her heart from any more pain. Her attention was momentarily caught by a spot on the far corner of the ceiling. It looked like it might be from a roof leak, but she didn't care.

It felt so strange not to care about the spot or the leak that might have caused it, and she wondered if she could possibly ever go about her daily life again carrying this much sadness.

She must have dozed, or perhaps she was simply sunk in such despair that the knock on the cabin door did not register, but the next thing she knew, Jack was standing over her, looking down at her with a puzzled expression on his face.

"Are you sick?" he asked.

"Go away, Jack."

He ignored her request. "What's wrong with you?"

"How did you find me?" She sat up. Being caught in Ben's bed in the middle of the morning was embarrassing.

"I needed to ask you about some supplies. Your truck was at the lodge, but you weren't in there. One of your guests said they thought they saw you go into Cabin 10." He glanced around. "Where's Ben?"

"I took him to the Chi-Cheemaun a little while ago."

"Why?"

"He's going back to Brazil; to the Yahnowa tribe."

"But we aren't finished with the lighthouse yet."

"I don't think that mattered," she said. "He told me that he knew you and I would make sure it got finished."

"Is he coming back?"

"He said he would... someday." Moriah felt a lump form in her throat.

The lump grew bigger and she couldn't control it. Before she knew it, she was sobbing out the whole sad story.

"Let me see if I've got this straight," Jack said. "You love him, and he loves you. The only thing you have to do in order to be together is get over this I-can't-leave-the-island thing?"

Moriah sniffed. "I guess that's about it."

"Then," Jack said. "You need to get over it."

"Seriously? That's the best you got? You don't think I don't *know* that?" Minutes ago she'd been sobbing into his shirt. Now she felt like smacking him. In some ways Jack could be so dense. "Overcoming a phobia is not easy!"

"Neither is beating alcoholism," Jack said.

"I'm sure it isn't, but what does that have to do with me and Ben?"

"I've found that going to Alcoholics Anonymous helps a lot."

"It isn't the same. They don't have AA for what I'm dealing with."

"Probably not," Jack said. "Maybe there's something else that would help."

"Like what?" She wiped her eyes and nose on Ben's sheet, figuring she'd be stuffing it into the lodge washing machine pretty soon anyway.

"I don't know." Jack shrugged. "I'm not any good with stuff like this. I'm thinking maybe a shrink or something?"

Moriah felt a little hurt. "You think I need a shrink?"

"Having to live on a small chunk of land for the rest of your life for no particular reason might be an indication."

"There's one problem with that solution."

"What?"

"There aren't any shrinks on Manitoulin Island. At least not yet."

"Maybe you could import one."

"Shrinks don't do house calls. I think you have to go to their office and lay on a couch or something."

"Too bad." Jack rose and headed for the door. "I liked Ben. So did Alicia."

After Jack left, Moriah flopped back down against the pillows and stared at the spot on the ceiling again. She didn't usually stop in the middle of the day for more than a moment or two, but today she needed to think and to think hard. Ben's abrupt departure had blindsided her.

Over the next hour, she deliberately and carefully came up with a plan. When she was finished, she threw back the covers, stripped the bed, dumped the linens in the laundry basket, slung Ben's rucksack of notebooks over her shoulder and marched up to the lodge.

The first thing she did was place Ben's translation notebooks high on a shelf in her closet. She would deal with those later. Then she stuffed the linens into the washing machine and watched the hot water rush in.

She had created this upstairs laundry room out of an unused closet, hanging the drywall, installing the clothes dryer and washer, making shelves the right width and length to store all the bedsheets and towels they needed for the resort. . It looked nice, and everything worked.

She had fixed nearly everything that was broken around the resort for years as well as making new out of old. But she had done all of it while walking around wounded. Moriah was tired of being broken, of limping through life. Tired of having faulty circuits running through her brain. She had no idea how to rewire herself, but on the rare times something broke around the resort that she didn't know how to fix, she had called in an expert.

She left the washing machine filling up and headed out the door.

Jack was right. It was high time she called for expert help.

Chapter Two

....

"I need a shrink." She burst into the doctor's private office.

"I told her she needed an appointment..." The nurse said, behind her.

The doctor looked confused. "But, I'm a pediatrician."

"I know," Moriah said. "You were my doctor when I was little. Do you remember when I was five and came back from South America after my parents were killed?"

He peered at her more closely. "Aren't you Katherine Robertson's niece?"

"The child who didn't talk for two years?" Moriah said. "Yep. That's me."

"But you did start to speak again. It just took some time. I heard that you were doing fine." He fiddled with a paperweight contrived of miniature golf clubs. Moriah noticed that his hands shook. "Why do you think you need a shr... a psychologist?"

"Because I'm *not* doing fine." Moriah put both of her hands flat on his desk and leaned toward him, keeping her voice low and steady. "I can't cross a bridge. I can't fly in a plane. I can't cross the gangplank onto the ferry. I have nightmares. I need help and I don't know who to contact."

"Check with my office staff. They might have a list of numbers you can try." He unclipped his stethoscope and stuffed it into his top drawer.

"You'll have to excuse me. Morning office hours are over and I need to go home."

Moriah, stunned, stood back and let him pass. There were other doctors on the island she could have approached, but she had been so physically healthy as an adult that she had never needed to see one. This was the only doctor she knew. Her memories of him were ones of kindness. His abrupt departure stung.

"He really is a good doctor," the nurse whispered behind her, "but he has the beginning stages of Parkinson's and tires easily. He wants to retire and there isn't anyone to take his place."

"I'm truly sorry about that, but I need some answers."

"Come to the front office," the nurse held the door open for her. "I might have some information I can give you."

"A list of shrinks?" Moriah cocked an eyebrow.

"No. More than that. My cousin suffered from severe panic attacks too," the nurse said. "She tried a lot of different therapies and therapists, but eventually found one who really helped. She said the therapist was a little different in her methods, but they worked."

The nurse found the number in the office Rolodex, scribbled it on a card and handed it to her.

"Where is he located?" Moriah asked.

"He's a she."

"Where is she located?"

"Cleveland, Ohio," the nurse said. "But I doubt she'll be willing to work with a patient over the phone."

"Actually," Moriah pocketed the number. "I was wondering if she liked to fish."

Chapter Three

The voice that greeted Moriah on the phone was low, warm and cultured. Unfortunately, she had gotten the psychologist's answering machine. The voice explained that the doctor was out of the office, but gave a number to call if it was an emergency.

Moriah considered for a moment. Yes. This was an emergency. Twenty years of nightmares and panic attacks and watching the man she loved sail away from her was definitely an emergency.

She dialed the number.

The same calm voice answered, but this time it was not a recording, and there were children's voices in the background.

"Dr. Crystal Barrett here, may I help you?"

Crystal? Moriah wondered how skilled of a psychologist she could be with a name like Crystal. It sounded like a better name for a head cheerleader.

"Excuse me," Dr. Barrett said, when Moriah didn't immediately respond. "Is anyone there?"

"Umm, yes. It's me." Moriah found her voice." I mean, my name is Moriah Robertson and I'm calling from Manitoulin Island, Canada."

"Robertson. I don't remember a Moriah Robertson. Are you a patient of mine?"

"No. But I want to be."

"I'm so sorry. You'll need to call my office tomorrow. I don't have my appointment calendar with me."

The voice was kind, even though it sounded as though Moriah had interrupted the family's dinner. She could hear cutlery and the scrapping of plates. Childish voices drifted over the phone, mixed with a man's.

"I can't make an appointment to come see you, Dr. Barrett. I can't leave this island." She clung to the receiver. This wasn't going to work. But it *had* to work. It simply had to.

Her heart was pounding hard and she broke out in a cold sweat as she tried to think of what to say next.

"I have money." Then she banged her forehead with her palm. What a nutcase she must sound. Dr. Crystal was probably used to getting weird phone calls from people during supper, but Moriah really hated being one of them.

Dr. Crystal shushed the children before she spoke again. "You can't leave the island?"

"Not since I was five."

"But, I live in Cleveland."

"Here's the deal." Moriah leaned her forehead against the wall. "I own a resort, Dr. Barrett. It's a lovely place. People even travel from foreign countries to stay with us. I was hoping you and your family would like to come and have a nice vacation? A week. A month. No charge. There's a playground for the children and I can show your husband all the best fishing spots. I'll pay you for your time too."

She hated the note of begging that had crept into her voice.

There was total silence on the other end of the phone and Moriah wondered if the doctor had hung up. She wouldn't blame her.

"It's called Robertson's Resort." Moriah tried to lend a little more legitimacy to her offer. "It's a real place. There's a lighthouse nearby that we're in the process of restoring this summer."

More silence while Moriah waited and watched the second hand tick away on the clock in front of her. Then finally...

"Moriah, I don't know you or what your issues are, but I'm going to take a leap of faith here and tell you that something remarkable may have happened. My husband and I had a two-week vacation planned with our children. It's rare that he and I can coordinate our schedules to have time off together and the children were so excited about our vacation. But the owners of the condominium we had rented at Myrtle Beach called and cancelled today. Something about plumbing issues."

Moriah gasped, threw her hand over her mouth, and clung to the receiver as the room spun around her.

"My husband does love to fish." There was a smile in the doctor's voice. "He rarely gets a chance. Where did you say this place is again?"

"Manitoulin Island. It's the largest freshwater island in the world and our resort is on the far south side of the island, right on Lake Huron."

"Give me a minute to ask my husband what he thinks."

Moriah heard muffled voices.

"We have three children." Dr. Barrett came back on the phone. "Is there room?"

"Yes!" Her voice was ragged with hope and excitement. "I'll have my best cabin ready for you. It has two bedrooms, a kitchen, and a couch in the front room that pulls out into a good bed. It's right on the beach and it has the most gorgeous view."

"Can it be ready a week from now?"

"It was ready yesterday."

"Please don't take offense, but Mike wants to do a little research into your resort first."

"I totally understand," Moriah said. "Tell him to call the Chamber of Commerce here on Manitoulin. They'll vouch for me."

"We'll do that," Crystal said. "But I have a strong feeling we might be meeting one another soon."

Moriah gave her the phone number of the resort and started to hang up when the doctor's voice stopped her.

"I'm very good at what I do, Moriah. There's a real chance that I can help you, but two weeks doesn't give us much time. You will need to work hard."

"Trust me, doctor," Moriah said. "If there is one thing I know how to do, it is how to work hard."

Based on the encouragement that Moriah heard in the doctor's voice, she decided to do something she wouldn't have dreamed of doing even a month earlier. She got in her truck and headed over to the post office on Mira Street. It was time to begin the process of getting a passport. Owning one had suddenly become as important to her as her purchase of the giant globe she kept in her bedroom.

Chapter Four

. . . .

"Hi." One week later Dr. Crystal Barrett jumped out of the white SUV and extended her hand. "I'm Crystal. You must be Moriah?"

The woman was so tiny, Moriah could hardly believe she had given birth to the three children she and her husband had brought with them.

Crystal had chestnut brown hair curling down her back, khaki Capri's, a cropped red shirt and matching red flip-flops. She also had the kindest brown eyes Moriah had ever seen. How could this elfin woman help her?

"Your cabin is down there," she pointed. "Number 10."

"John, would you mind?"

"Got it covered, babe." A tall, good-looking man was standing beside the van. "Take your time."

He climbed in and started the motor. Three elementary school-age children were busy chattering together in the back.

Crystal touched Moriah's arm.

"John and the children will be fine. It was nice of you to invite us. It's been a long ride and I'm tired of sitting. Would you like to show me around your island while he and the children get everything unpacked?"

"It's a really big island."

"Then let's start with the lighthouse, I've always wanted to see one up close."

It was the exact right thing to say. Moriah had been feeling awkward about opening up to a stranger, so she was happy to have the task of showing Crystal the work they were doing on the lighthouse.

Soon, they were finished with the tour and Moriah found herself sitting on the cottage steps watching the sunset with her newest guest. The awkwardness was gone. The lovely, young doctor had somehow become a friend.

"I can certainly see why you love this place so much," Crystal said. "I can feel its power. Manitoulin Island is a healing place."

"It's always seemed that way to me," Moriah said.

"This is an especially lovely spot. It might be a good place to start telling me what's in your heart," Crystal said. "If you want."

"Like what should I say?" Moriah asked. "I don't know how to do this."

"Start at the beginning," Crystal said. "And tell me everything that's bothering you. I can listen for a really long time."

No one, not even Ben, had known the right questions to ask, the right moment to stay silent, the right verbal prompt to get her started again. This fairy-like woman *did* know. Moriah didn't just tell the doctor what was in her heart, she poured out her guts. Even *she* was surprised at how many words she had bottled up inside of her. Crystal quietly listened to every last one.

Finally, as the last rays of the sun disappeared, Moriah simply ran out of words. All her worries, fears and bad memories had been deposited at Dr. Barrett's flip-flop clad feet. Crystal now sat, chin on fist, one foot tapping, lost in thought.

"I think that's about it." Moriah awkwardly came to the end of her life story.

"Probably not, but it's a good start. Do you feel any better?"

Moriah mentally examined herself. "Yeah. I guess I do. Sort of."

"Takes some of the pressure off when one gets to truly talk. It's like lancing a boil."

"I've never had a boil."

"Me either." Crystal laughed. "I've never even lanced one. It's mainly just something people say. A boil is quite painful though, and lancing it helps drain all the poison out so the body can heal itself. Talking honestly to someone often does the same thing; helps drain some of the toxins from the mind so it can begin to heal."

The doctor stood and brushed off the seat of her Capri's.

"I'm going to think about everything you've said tonight. You'll need to go to work tomorrow and I'll have fun fishing with Mike and playing with the kids. Let's plan to get together tomorrow evening and see what insights God provides. I'll meet you back here."

Chapter Five

With renewed enthusiasm fueled entirely by hope, Moriah threw herself back into the work at the lighthouse the next day.

"You doing okay?" Jack buckled on his tool belt.

"Yes." Moriah tied a handkerchief around her forehead to keep the sweat from getting in her eyes. "And if Ben comes back—excuse me—*when* Ben comes back, I want to have everything about this lighthouse finished and ready to show him."

"Have you heard anything from him?"

"He called from the Toronto airport to tell me he had gotten there safely. That's the last I talked with him."

"What about Katherine and Nicolas?"

"Got one phone call from the Cayman Islands." Moriah grinned. "Katherine sounded all giggly."

"It's hard to imagine Katherine giggly," Jack said. "I suppose we can assume the honeymoon is going well?"

"Sounded like it to me."

"If anyone deserves a nice honeymoon, it's Katherine."

"I agree. Nicolas is not my cup of tea, but he seems to be exactly what Katherine has waited for all these years."

"No accounting for taste." Jack drew on his work gloves. "Alicia picking me, for instance."

"Or Ben picking me."

"He's a smart man, Moriah. He knows a good thing when he sees it."

"You suppose?"

"Suppose nothing. Nobody miters corners like you do. Now help me get this lumber off the truck. The foghorn room is not going to remodel itself, you know."

* * *

It was a two-day trek into the rainforest to reach the boundaries of the Yahnowa. Ben's clothes were either soaked or damp for the entire two days. This was nothing new to him. He was used to living wet in the jungle and had learned long ago to ignore the discomfort. That was something easily endured, but the ache of being separated from Moriah was nearly intolerable.

His mind was so occupied with the image of Moriah crying and falling to her knees, as the ferry took him away from her, and the waves pounded against the rocky Canadian shore, that his first glimpse of the Yahnowa village felt dreamlike. The scene before him of fragile huts, smoking cook fires and naked children seemed unreal, like something lifted out of the pages of a magazine.

Then he saw Abraham and Violet sweltering beneath the shade of their loosely thatched porch.

"Hello, Ben." Violet remained where she was, seated on a bench.

Normally, she would jump up and greet him with a hug. This time she could only manage a weak smile.

"What are you two still doing here?" he asked. "I thought you were going home."

"Violet was not strong enough to leave on foot," Abraham explained, with a quick, worried glance at his wife.

It was obvious to Ben that Violet had kept her secret far too long. He was shocked at how feeble she had grown over the summer. He understood now why Abraham sounded so desperate on the phone.

"She didn't tell me." Abraham said later, after drawing Ben aside. "She kept hoping the problem would go away. She didn't want to keep me from my work."

"How long has she suspected?"

"Since the week before you left."

"I could have taken her with me!" Ben groaned. "I could have gotten her to a good hospital."

"I know," Abraham said. "Trust me, that thought has been keeping me up at night."

"So, what's the plan?"

"When I trekked out to make that phone call to you, I looked up Ron Meacham. His helicopter has been out of commission for a while. It takes a lot of time and effort to track down parts for that old Huey of his, but he says he thinks he'll have it ready within the next couple of days. Some of the villagers have been clearing a space big enough to set it down."

"Thank God for the Christian Pilot's Association," Ben said.

"Truly," Abraham said. "They are such a lifeline."

"You and Violet will be sipping sweet iced tea with your son in Alabama in no time."

"Ben." Abraham's face was grim. "I don't think Violet and I will be coming back."

The two men had been close for far too long for Ben to fall back on platitudes.

"I know, brother." Ben placed a comforting hand on the older man's shoulder.

"I don't think I could bear it if you weren't here to continue our work." Abraham searched Ben's face. "You will stay, won't you, son?

You'll see this work through?"

Ben's heart was heavy as he made the promise he knew Abraham desperately needed to hear.

"Yes, Abraham. I'll stay."

Chapter Six

....

The evening sessions with Crystal were often painful. The woman used questions as skillfully as a surgeon wielded a scalpel.

Moriah was shocked to discover that she had clearly seen Chief Moawa's face. That painted mask of murderous intent was permanently etched in her mind. In fact, she came to realize that all the boogeymen of her childhood had worn Moawa's face. Her childhood monsters weren't nebulous or imagined. Hers had been real. Too real.

As they sat at the lodge's dining room table, Crystal handed her a blank piece of paper.

"Moriah, can you draw?"

"Not well, but I took a couple art classes in high school."

"Good." She handed her a pencil. "I want you to draw a picture of Chief Moawa."

"I don't think I can."

"Try," Crystal said. "What color hair did he have?"

"Black, of course," Moriah said. "Everyone had black hair except some of the very old."

"So, start with that." Crystal pushed a small box of crayons toward her. "Use color if it will help."

When Moriah finished, even though the sketch was rough, she stared at a frightening, painted face, full of evil. She had no idea if it was the least bit correct, but it was a fairly accurate representation of her childhood memory.

Crystal looked over her shoulder. "Scares the dickens out of me. I'd wet the bed if that guy showed up in my nightmares. You think he still looks like this? Twenty years can take the juice out of a man. Even a bad man."

"Doesn't matter. His face will always be the same to me."

"You ever wonder if he's still alive?"

"I never thought much about it. Why?"

"Maybe you could go see him sometime and tell him what he did to you."

"Go meet him?" Moriah shuddered. "Not in this lifetime. Not ever."

"Seriously," Crystal tapped the picture with her finger. "It would be nice if you could find out if this particular boogeyman still exists."

"I don't have a clue how to find that out," Moriah said.

"Does Ben know?"

"I never asked him."

"Ask him sometime." Crystal held the picture at arm's length, then laid it back on the table. "In the meantime, let's see what we can do with this."

Crystal chose a black crayon from the box and started sketching on Chief Moawa's picture, her tongue clamped between her teeth in concentration. As the picture began to change, Moriah burst into astonished laughter. Moawa now bore a strong resemblance to Mad Magazine's "What Me Worry?" picture of Alfred E. Newman. A tooth was missing, his ears stuck straight out, and a shock of hair fell over one eye.

Crystal had taken evil and made it look goofy.

"Tape this picture to your bedroom wall and every time you feel a boogeyman attack coming on look at this and laugh."

"This will work?"

"Maybe. At least a little bit," Crystal said. "I have one on my wall at home, too."

Moriah stared at her friend in surprise. "You have a boogeyman?"

"Actually, I think of him as a giant. Did you ever hear the story of the giants who were so terrifying to the people of Israel they were afraid to cross the Jordan River into the Promised Land?"

"I know the story."

"For me, the giant was a man in our neighborhood who liked little girls way too much and very inappropriately."

"Oh no. I'm so sorry, Crystal."

"Me too. Over the years, I've discovered nearly everyone has a giant of some sort in their life. It's not always a person. Sometimes, it's a habit they want to break, or a handicap they have to overcome. Sometimes nothing more than negative words they heard in childhood that they continue to replay over and over without even realizing they're doing it."

"But you're so strong."

Crystal laughed at that with such abandon that Moriah feared she would fall out of her chair. Finally, she sobered up enough to speak.

"You have no idea how much stronger you are than I used to be, Moriah. You managed to have a whole, large island as your personal boundary. I did fine for a while, stuffed my memories down deep, attended college and made good grades." She smiled. "I even got an advanced degree in psychology. Then, shortly after the birth of my second child, I became reluctant to go outside my house. It was my haven. Then I began to spend more time in my bedroom. It was upstairs and it felt safer than, say, the kitchen or living room."

Crystal absently stirred her cup of cooling tea with one finger.

"It wasn't until my husband found me sitting in my closet with the door closed, our two older children watching cartoons on our bed, and our third baby on my lap, that he forced me to seek help. It was hard, but I fought my way out of that dark place and have been helping others ever since."

"You fix broken people." Moriah understood completely. "I fix broken things."

"You also build new with good materials, and the things you build are strong and not easily broken. I'm raising children who will, hopefully, never feel the need to sit in a closet as an adult with the door shut. I'm teaching others how to do the same. You will build a good life, Moriah. Whether here, or in the rainforest. As motivated as you are, and with some of the tools I'll give you, you'll build a life as strong and filled with purpose as… as that lighthouse you've put so much care into."

Moriah gazed out of the window at the lake and the gleaming tower. "I like the sound of that, Crystal, and I love the silly picture of Moawa. But what about the bridge? Drawing a funny picture of the bridge won't help me. How do I get across it without feeling like I'm having a heart attack?"

"One step at a time, like everything else. A major tool I'm going to teach you to use is desensitization."

"Desensitization?"

"Let me explain it by telling you a story. Did you ever hear of an author by the name of Marjorie Kinnan Rawlings?"

"I'm not much of a reader."

"Doesn't matter. Rawlings wrote a famous book called *The Yearling.*"

Moriah shook her head. She had never heard of it.

"It was made into a movie many years ago."

"I don't have a lot of time to watch movies."

Crystal sighed. "It doesn't matter. What matters is that Marjorie bought an orange grove in Florida and moved there from New York City."

Although Moriah didn't spend a lot of time reading, she did like a good story, especially if it ended with something she could use to cross the bridge. She settled back against her chair, ready to listen.

"Did she like Florida?"

"She loved it. Absolutely loved it. Felt like it was the one place on earth where she truly belonged. Except for one thing."

"What was that?"

"Marjorie was terrified of snakes."

Moriah shuddered. "I can understand that. I've heard there are some bad snakes in Florida."

"Yes, there are, and while Marjorie waited and worked and tried to get published, she supported herself by growing oranges. But there was a problem. Florida farmers can't afford to be too afraid of snakes. She had to get over her fear if she was going to run an orange grove."

"What did she do?"

"She desensitized herself. There were professional rattlesnake hunters in the area, men who made their living hunting, selling and collecting venom. She asked permission to go out with them on a hunt."

"I'd die."

"Marjorie thought she would too, but she was a determined woman. She loved her farm and needed to be able to take care of it without running into the house and cowering in her bed every time she saw a snake. She loved the farm so much she was willing to fight against her fear."

Moriah was pretty sure she knew where Crystal was going with this story.

"She spent several days on that hunt. During which, she saw the men capture and handle dozens of snakes. Marjorie got to see more snakes than she had ever seen in her life. By the end of the hunt, she had stopped jumping out of her skin each time one crossed her path. Eventually, she was able to catch and handle them herself. After that she was never afraid again."

"A bridge isn't a snake."

"Same principle though. You'll need to become so familiar with the bridge that all its power over you will drain away."

"I'll do anything if it means getting to be with Ben."

"Good, because great love can conquer great fear. Fighting this because of your love for Ben is a good thing, but it might not be enough," Crystal said. "How do you feel about yourself? Do you love yourself enough to do this?"

Moriah squirmed a little, uncomfortable with the question. "I don't know. That sounds a little self-centered."

"Then let me phrase it differently. Do you ever dislike or hate yourself?"

Moriah thought about that.

"Sometimes."

"So many people feel that way. Women especially. Maybe it's a societal thing, I don't know. What I do know is that self-hatred can severely use up a person's strength and weaken their courage."

"So, what am I supposed to do?"

"Let's try an exercise that I have found helpful. Do you know any five-year-old girls?"

"Yes. Alicia's little sister, Emma. She's adorable."

"Innocent? Loving? Trusting?"

"Oh yes."

"Do you love her?"

"It would be hard not to love Emma."

"Okay then," Crystal said. "I want you to close your eyes. Imagine Emma having to see the same things you saw that terrible night. What does it make you want to do?"

"I want to shield her and run away with her to safety."

"You can do that now. For yourself."

Moriah opened her eyes. "I don't understand."

"Let me try to explain. There is a little girl who wants to be safe and loved hidden inside of every woman. Sometimes that child has gone through more than any child should have to endure. Instead of protecting that precious little girl, many of us spend our lives beating up on her. Because we were abused, we continue to abuse the child within us without even realizing we are doing it."

Crystal handed Moriah a small pillow from the couch. "Hold this in your arms for now. Close your eyes again. This time, I want you to go down deep. I want you to imagine wiping the tears from that little five-year-old face that used to be yours. Pretend that you are cradling her in your arms."

Moriah tried to envision her own face as a child. There was a photo that Katherine had taken soon after her parents died. She had been a pretty little girl with delicate features, dressed in a flowered blue dress. Her long hair was tied up with two matching bows. There was a Christmas tree in the background, and a pile of presents in front of her, but she wasn't smiling. Instead her eyes were fearful as she looked at the camera and her face was troubled.

As she thought about that frightened little girl, Moriah held the pillow closer to her chest and began to rock slightly.

"Tell her it's going to be okay," Crystal said. "Tell her that you are all grown-up now. You're big and strong and, from this point on, you will take really good care of her. Say it aloud."

Moriah opened her eyes and looked at Crystal. "Are you sure about this?"

"Trust me," Crystal said. "This is important."

Moriah tried to do as Crystal said. She went deep. In her mind, she looked down into that small, frightened face. That innocent child had gone through such a terrible experience. No one deserved to go through that.

"It wasn't your fault," Moriah began. "You didn't do anything wrong."

She stopped. Looked at Crystal, who nodded encouragement. Moriah closed her eyes again. Held the pillow a little closer.

"It wasn't your fault that those bad men hurt your parents. You were a brave little girl. You tried to run to them. You fought to get out of the hut and tried to scream at the bad men to stop, but Akawe held you back. He knew you couldn't do anything to save them. It wasn't your fault that you survived. Akawe saved your life. You were exactly where your mommy and daddy wanted you to be—where you *needed* to be. Safe in Akawe's house."

"Go on," Crystal whispered.

"You'll go through some scary things, but you will be okay."

Scene after horrific scene ran through her mind as a feeling of protectiveness washed over her toward the little girl she had once been. Yes, it was easy to love the damaged child who had grown up to become her own flawed self.

"I'm big and strong now," Moriah continued. "I'm all grown up and I can protect you now. You didn't deserve to go through what happened. You deserve to grow up and have a good life. You deserve to be loved."

"People can do amazingly courageous things for someone they love," Crystal said. "Your love for Ben is strong and it might be enough, but I'm thinking you'll also need love for yourself—for that hurt little girl within you—to break through the barrier of crossing that bridge so you can give her a normal life. Promise her that you will love her and fight for her."

"I love you." Hot tears began to course down her cheeks. "And I promise to fight hard for you as long as I live."

Crystal gave her the space she needed to cry for her lost childhood.

Chapter Seven

As Moriah dressed for work the next morning, she felt like there had been a subtle shift deep within her. Everything felt a little brighter, a little lighter, and she could hardly wait to start her day.

Early morning sunlight glinted off the new windows of the foghorn room across the lake. She had made a dramatic change in her original plan for the large room that had once connected the lighthouse cottage with the tower and she was enormously proud of the result.

The foghorn room had sustained the greatest part of the steam explosion that created the crack in the light tower. One whole wall had been destroyed with that explosion. Originally, she had planned to rebuild the outer wall as it had once been. Then, the idea came to her that filling that space with a wall of windows would be an even better idea. By the time she finished drawing up plans, the walls on both sides were filled with the most durable windows money could buy.

It was going to be a lovely, large room that would not only give people a magnificent view, but would capture the limited sunlight that Manitoulin Island received in the winter. Plants would thrive in that room. Whoever got to live in the lighthouse was going to love spending time there.

The lantern room at the top of the tower was coming along nicely. It was all so beautiful—a feast for her eyes and a balm to her heart.

She tore her gaze away from the window and finished getting

dressed. As usual, the last thing she did before leaving her room was give the giant globe a spin. Then she closed her eyes and rested her finger lightly on the surface as it spun.

When the globe stopped spinning, the country of Brazil lay beneath her finger.

She had not expected that. Often, she ended up somewhere out in the ocean, but today her finger had stopped in the middle of the Amazon rainforest.

Superstition was not one of her weaknesses. She knew there was nothing magical about the huge globe upon which she had spent a month's income. Spinning it and thinking about visiting one of those countries was just a game. She was only pretending that she would one day be able to visit those places.

Today, however, it did seem to be an omen. What was it that Crystal had said last night? Great love could overcome great fear?

If that was true, and she had faith that it was, there was no doubt in her mind that she would someday be able to go to Ben.

Of course, there was still that blasted bridge to cross, but for the first time ever she knew she would conquer it. It wouldn't be easy, and it might not happen all at once, but it *would* happen. For Ben, for her, and for that little girl still within her she would cross it.

In the meantime, she still had a resort to run.

Alicia was already at the lodge and perched on a high stool behind the reception desk when Moriah went downstairs. Little Betsy was napping, snuggled into a stretchy blue wrap that Alicia used when she was working. It freed both of her hands, one of which held a phone to her ear, while the other one patted Betsy's tiny bottom.

"Thanks, yes, I'll tell her." Alicia hung up.

"Tell me what?" Moriah said.

"That was Tom Hawkins; the guy who has been working on the old desk that was in the lighthouse."

"Is he finished?" Moriah asked, eagerly.

"Yes. He said to have a couple men from your crew to come pick it up tomorrow, but he said for you to make sure and come with them."

"Why?"

"He said there's something he wants to show you."

"That's intriguing," Moriah said. "Anything else I need to know before I head out to the worksite?"

"The guests in cabins eight and six are leaving this morning. We don't have those two cabins reserved for anyone else at present. My guess is that we can start shutting them down for winter. I'm not sure we have enough toilet paper to get us through to the end of the season. Do you want me to order another box?"

"Yes," Moriah said. "And that reminds me. We need to have the septic tank checked soon. I don't want to risk any overflows. Can you call Amos Bradshaw for me?"

"Got it." Alicia jotted something on a notepad.

"I'm starting to wonder what we did around here without you," Moriah said.

"Me too!" Alicia grinned. "I really appreciate the job. It's great to be able to bring my baby to work with me."

At that moment Betsy awoke, poked her little head out of the wrap and gave Moriah a rosy, sleepy smile. She had her father's blonde hair and it was tousled from being inside the wrap.

"That baby is such a hit with the guests," Moriah said. "I think we might have to put her on the payroll too."

Thanks to Alicia, she felt like she could leave the resort, even with Katherine and Nicolas gone, with a clear mind. Hiring Jack's wife was one of the best things she'd done this summer. The young woman looked after the resort as though it were her own.

SERENA B. MILLER

As Moriah drove out to the worksite, she thought about the desk that Liam Robertson had built. She looked forward to seeing what Tom had done with it. She couldn't remember a time when it wasn't scarred and blackened with the slow accumulation of grime. It was so heavy, it would take two strong men to help her lift it into the truck. Jack said the thing weighed well over three-hundred pounds and it was an awkward shape.

She had not heard from Ben in over a week. He had called once after landing in South America—then silence. She imagined him trekking through the jungle now, or maybe arriving at the Yahnowa village. It was maddening not to know what was happening.

She recalled the conversation they had the evening before he left.

"When I finish my work for the Yahnowa," he had told her. "I intend to leave nothing behind except a good translation of the Scripture, and what language skills I can give them. Other than that, the Smiths and I are determined to leave their culture intact."

"In what way?" Moriah asked.

"We've never encouraged them to wear modern clothing. In the circumstances and weather they live in, their near nudity makes sense. It's always wet in the rainforest. While the Smiths and I are walking around in wet, steaming clothes, the Yahnowa are quite comfortable. In the past, some missionaries did a lot of damage in trying to change everything about the people to whom they were trying to minister. We've learned the hard way over the years to respect the wisdom of the elders, and to pay attention to their medicine men. Sometimes they know things we do not. Of course, sometimes we know things they don't. It is good to listen to one another."

"So, you don't try to change anything?"

"The killing of people in other tribes. We've tried hard to stop that. There are unique tribes in the Amazon with as few as thirty people.

41

It doesn't take much for a larger and stronger group like the Yahnowa to destroy a group that small. Teaching them about a loving God who expects them to also be loving, helps."

"What about the clinic Nicolas' mother established?" she asked. "Will you ever try to bring it back?"

"That's what Nicolas intends to do if he can find the right medical personnel to staff it. I know the Yahnowa would be grateful for a doctor and nurse to be available. There are so many mishaps and diseases in the jungle."

That had worried her. "You will be careful, won't you?"

"Me?" Ben had laughed. "Of course I will. 'Careful' is my middle name."

"Seriously," Moriah had said. "I've seen some of the terrible things that live there. I had a flashback of watching an Anaconda slithering across the path. I was sitting on Petras' shoulders at the time. Even he was frightened."

"Oh, Moriah." He had given her a hug. "If an Anaconda swallowed me, I'd taste so bad he'd spit me back out. Pray for me, but please promise you'll stop worrying."

So, she had promised, but she knew it would be a lot easier to keep that promise if she could be there to watch out for him.

That afternoon, with all sort of hope and courage and resolve flooding her heart, hoping to be able to tell Crystal that she had succeeded, she went to visit the bridge again. This time she knew absolutely that she could cross it. Two hours later she drove home, drained and shaking.

She had been wrong.

Chapter Eight

....

"I've been thinking," Crystal said, as they sat across from each other at the kitchen table that night, each with a cup of tea in front of them. Crystal also had an extra notebook and pen with her.

"Your reaction the day you found out the truth about how your parents died doesn't seem healthy to me," Crystal said.

"Healthy?" Moriah said.

"'Authentic' might be a better word."

"Are you trying to avoid using the word 'normal,' Crystal?"

"Doesn't matter." Crystal waved the question away. "From what I understand, you absorbed the fact of your parents' murder, and of Katherine lying about it, and then simply went on with your work."

"What else was I supposed to do?" Moriah asked. "Katherine was only trying to protect me, and I can't change the fact of my parent's deaths."

Crystal didn't say anything.

"I had work to do," Moriah continued. "I needed to move on."

Crystal still didn't say anything.

"What?" Moriah asked, defensively.

"You stuffed your anger and grief down as deep as possible so you could go on," Crystal said. "It's quite admirable. People do it all the time. So, in that case, yes, I suppose you could say that it's 'normal.' But that doesn't mean it's healthy."

"What should I have done? Thrown a temper tantrum? I can't change anything that happened now. Katherine just did the best she could."

Crystal scooted the notebook and pen across the table toward her.

"I want you to write a letter?"

"To Katherine?"

"No, dear. I want you to write a letter to your mother."

"My *mother*? How will that help?"

"Tell her all that you remember about her. If you feel like it, tell her how much you miss her."

Moriah did not like to write letters.

"I hate to say this, Crystal, but that sounds like a waste of time."

Crystal's eyes snapped. "Do you consider anything else I've asked you to do a waste of time?"

"No."

"Then go find a comfortable spot and write the letter."

Moriah reluctantly took the notebook and pen into the living room to an old leather chair by the window. She expected the psychologist to leave but Crystal had brought a paperback with her and settled down onto the couch.

"What are you reading?" Moriah asked.

"A book on sociopaths," Crystal said.

"Doesn't sound like vacation reading."

"It is to me."

"Have you ever worked with a sociopath?"

"Moriah! You are avoiding the assignment I gave you. Stop distracting yourself from your task. You know you don't give a flip about what I'm reading."

With a huge sigh, Moriah opened the notebook and clicked the pen.

Dear Mom,

I'm sorry that you died. I wish you were here.

Love,

Moriah

She tore the page out and handed it to Crystal who glanced at it.

"Seriously, Moriah?"

"I was five. I barely knew the woman."

"Try again." Crystal crumpled the letter and tossed it into a nearby trashcan. "Think back. What can you remember about your mom? Was she pretty? Was she strict? Did she cuddle you when you fell? What colors do you remember her wearing? Did she sing lullabies to you? Think, Moriah. Five-year-olds have memories. What do you remember about living here on Manitoulin with your parents before they took you to Brazil?"

Moriah leaned her head back against her armchair and tried to focus. It was hard. Had there been anything about her mother...

"Strawberries." Moriah said. "I remember my mom used a perfume that smelled like strawberries."

"Interesting," Crystal said.

"Why?"

"Because I've noticed that you often smell of strawberries too."

"I don't wear perfume."

"Is it your shampoo, perhaps?"

Moriah felt a little dizzy when she realized that the shampoo she preferred was always strawberry scented if she could find it.

"You're right," Moriah admitted. "As usual."

"I believe there might be more childhood memories there than you realized. What kind of hair did she have?"

"Long," Moriah said. "Curly. I remember playing with it. I liked to twist the curls around my finger."

"Was she kind to you?"

"I think so. I have a vague memory of baking cookies together. I remember sleeping in bed between her and dad one time when I was ill."

"How did you feel lying there between them?"

"Safe," Moriah said, without hesitation.

"Good. Do you remember any jewelry? Earrings, jangly bracelets? Things like that?"

"I remember she always wore a tiny cross on a necklace," Moriah said. "It was gold and delicate-looking. She didn't let me play with it, although I wanted to."

"I noticed a photo of an old woman in an oval frame on the wall of the kitchen. Who was that?"

"My great, great, grandmother, Eliza."

"The lighthouse keeper?"

"Yes."

"You don't resemble her much. Do you have any photos of your mother?"

"I don't think so. We have some old family photos of various grand-parents and my dad and Katherine when they were small. But Katherine said my parents took the photo albums with them that had photos of themselves and me the second time they went to help at the clinic. They wanted to show their Yahnowa friends about their life on Manitoulin Island. She said she never saw the albums again."

"So, you have no pictures of your mom and dad as adults?"

"I guess not."

"Interesting." Crystal closed her book. "It's time for me to get back to help put the kids to bed. I'll see you tomorrow evening."

"I apologize for not being excited about writing the letter."

"Some techniques work and some don't," Crystal said.

"I do appreciate your help," Moriah said.

"You're welcome, but I have a feeling you won't like me much after what I'm about to say."

"Really? Why?"

"I've never met your aunt, but I can't help wondering if Katherine was telling you the truth about those photo albums."

Moriah tried to go to sleep after Crystal left. She got ready for bed and climbed beneath the covers, but she couldn't help thinking about what Crystal had said.

She knew every inch of the lodge, except what was in Katherine's room. That was off-limits unless Katherine called her in to look or help her with something specific. After Moriah had grown up, Katherine afforded her the same courtesy. Their rooms were their own private spaces. It was important to have a private space when everything else at the resort was at the disposal of their guests. Now she kept tossing and turning, wondering if her beloved aunt had lied to her about something else. Was there any possibility that there were photos of her parents? If there were, the only place they could be hidden was in her room.

Katherine was in Cancun.

She did not feel good about it, but she knew she wouldn't get a moment's rest until she'd convinced herself that Katherine wasn't lying about the photos.

Reluctantly, she went to investigate her aunt's bedroom. Inviting someone like Crystal into your life surely did stir things up.

There weren't many places to hide a photo album in a room as sparse and clean as Katherine kept hers. The closet only held a few clothes and—surprise!—a box of old letters from Nicolas she'd saved all these years. Moriah had no trouble ignoring them.

The only space remaining in which something could be hidden was a large bureau. Moriah started at the top and worked her way down. There was not much there except for nightclothes and underwear. Nothing remarkable or out of the ordinary came to light. She was starting to feel relieved she had not found anything, until she opened the bottom drawer. There, hidden beneath a handmade quilt, were two thick photo albums.

With trembling hands, Moriah lifted them out and took them to the bed, where she sat and began to turn pages. She felt the blood drain from her face as she saw picture after picture of a happy family.

She realized that she was feeling quite cold. Unnaturally cold.

Throwing on her old, blue bathrobe, she took the albums downstairs and lit a fire in the fireplace. Then, still shivering from a coldness that seemed to be coming more from inside herself than the actual room temperature, she settled down to examine every picture.

There was a picture of her mother hugely pregnant and smiling. Sweet photos of her parents in the hospital cradling their new baby. Her on her first birthday with a demolished cake in front of her and vanilla icing all over her face. Page after page of family photos. They told the unmistakable story that she had been cherished.

The photos flooded her mind with wonderful, untapped, childhood memories. She always had a vague idea that her mother was pretty; now she saw that her mother was beautiful. Yet there was no preening or posing. Her mother seemed only to have eyes for her little girl and for Moriah's father.

The albums also contained the photos from their first trip to Dr. Janet's clinic. Moriah could see herself at four, playing in the dirt with the tribal children. A small, dark-haired girl was in the photo beside her. It was Karyona, her special friend with whom she had been staying with the night of the massacre.

About one o'clock in the morning, she closed the albums, carefully sat them on the side-table beside her chair, picked up Crystal's notebook and pen and began to write the letter she had requested.

"*Dear Mom and Dad,*

You were wonderful parents. I miss you both terribly..."

As dawn broke over the horizon she had managed to pour her heart onto approximately eleven notebook pages in a letter to her mother and father.

It had not been easy. Tears had fallen on those pages as she allowed herself to fully realize and absorb the impact of all she had lost. She was fairly certain she had cried more in the past couple of months than she had her whole life. By the time she finished her letter, her eyelids were hot and swollen, and she was nearly cross-eyed from fatigue.

It struck her that perhaps tonight she had begun to mourn her parents as a fully functioning adult should mourn, instead of a bewildered child.

With all her heart, she wished she had Ben here to discuss all this with, but she didn't, and she wouldn't for a long time unless she was able to overcome and process all these new things she was discovering.

Why had Katherine hidden these photos away from her for so long?

She had always loved and trusted her aunt. She still loved her aunt and always would but, after the silence about her and Nicolas' relationship, the lies about her parents' death, and then hiding the photo albums—her trust was running out.

Chapter Nine

Ron got his helicopter repaired in the nick of time. Violet was so sick, Ben was afraid that her death and burial might have to take place right there in the rainforest. He prayed for her and Abraham daily, but it was with a heavy heart. Everyone's life eventually came to an end, no matter how useful or faithful. That was just a fact of life. Still, it was hard to see those two old missionaries leave with Ron.

Alone in his hut, Ben assessed the situation. It would take him at least another year to finish the translation. Much longer than that if he took over the regimen of teaching and preaching that Abraham had kept up.

The village would miss Violet. She had been such a valiant soldier, working alongside the Yahnowa women, teaching them Bible lessons as they roasted plantain together or patted out the day's manioc cakes. He had even seen her hunt for the palm heart worms to which the Yahnowa were addicted, roasting them on a stick and feeding bits to whichever child happened to be on her lap.

Deep down, he realized that the greatest struggle for him wouldn't be the extra teaching he had to do, or the sleep he would need to miss if he were to finish the translation sooner. It was the loss of two people who had managed to be upbeat and happy as they'd worked together in a difficult mission field. Their encouragement had meant more to him than even he had realized.

He loved the Yahnowa, enjoyed working with them, and could possibly spend the rest of his life serving them. But not alone. He needed Moriah.

"Fight hard, my love," he whispered into the night. "Fight hard."

Chapter Ten

That evening after work, Moriah and Crystal drove to Little Current. The heavy, iron bridge loomed in the twilight, monstrous and menacing.

As always, bile rose in her throat but, while Crystal watched, Moriah grasped the handrail and began to inch along the bridge walkway, drawing on every bit of willpower she possessed. This time she was going to conquer it!

She made it several yards before she hit some sort of emotional wall. The next thing she knew, she was hanging her head over the bridge railing, throwing up.

Crystal was at her side in an instant, pressing a tissue into her shaking hand.

Moriah wiped her mouth with the tissue and crumpled it into her fist.

"That's enough." Crystal hugged her. "Let's go home."

They made their way back to Moriah's truck and sat for a long time, staring at the bridge.

"You tried too much, too fast." Crystal drummed her fingers on the seat. "Don't push yourself so far. Stop before you get to that point of panic. Go a few baby steps each time. Do only as much as you can comfortably bear. Are you listening?"

Moriah nodded. She was drained from the effort and wanted only to go home.

"You can overcome this, Moriah, I promise," Crystal said. "One step at a time, you can overcome this. Literally, one step at a time. It doesn't have to be a marathon. Take a few steps on it every day. If you let too much time pass between your attempts, the fear will have time to build up again. Desensitization. That's what we're going for. Familiarity. You *are* going to beat this."

Chapter Eleven

"You look like something the cat dragged in," Jack said, after she had climbed all the way to the top of the tower.

"That's something a girl wants to hear first thing in the morning," Moriah said. "I tried to cross the bridge again last night."

"I'm thinking it didn't go well?"

"Your thinking would be correct," Moriah said. "I need for you to come with me to Mindemoya to pick up Liam's desk. He called Alicia and left word that it was ready."

"Are you trying to give me a hernia?" Jack said. "I helped drag that monster over to Tom's last month. Maybe we could talk him into keeping it permanently."

"Tom also told Alicia that he has something to show me," Moriah said. "But he wouldn't tell her what."

"Hey, Luke," Jack called to one of the workmen sanding the wooden floor of the lantern room. "You want to come with us? We've got to go bring that desk back Tom's been working on."

Luke, a twenty-five year old First Nation workman, was a man of few words. "Sure."

The drive to Tom's in Mindemoya felt a bit crowded with two large, sweaty men sharing the seat with her. Without the possible cost of purchasing the lighthouse weighing on her anymore, she began to think seriously about the possibility of purchasing a newer, larger truck.

Tom's shop was built onto the side of a small barn which was badly in need of paint. He seemed nervous when they walked in.

"I hope you're happy with it," he said. "It was a challenge."

He pulled a tarp off the desk and Moriah caught her breath at the sight of the richly glowing walnut wood grain beneath. This was what had been hiding under the dust and dirt all these years? Her great-great-grandfather had certainly known his way around a good piece of lumber.

"It's lovely," she said. "You did a fantastic job."

"You gave me a key to the larger hidden compartment," he said. "But you didn't tell me that there was a hidden drawer. Did you know?"

"I had no idea."

"Let me show you." Tom got down on his knees and opened the large cedar-lined compartment. "You have to look close to see it."

Moriah knelt beside Tom as he grasped a knob so tiny she had never noticed it before. He tugged, and a small drawer slid out.

"There's something in there," Moriah said.

"Yes," he said. "That is what I wanted to show you."

He reached inside the drawer and handed her a small, cracked, red-leather book. "It's Eliza Robertson's diary."

"Seriously?" Moriah was awestruck as she opened it. On the flyleaf, written in old-fashioned, fancy penmanship were the words *"Eliza Robertson. Her diary. May 10, 1874."*

"It's been there all these years and no one knew?" Moriah's voice was reverent as she gently turned to the first page, feasting her eyes on line after line of cramped, old-fashioned handwriting. "Did you have a chance to read any of it?"

"No. I looked at the first page, but that sort of curlicued, spidery handwriting gives me a headache."

She stared at the first page for a moment, then turned it sideways. "It is oddly written. Is it in some sort of code do you think?"

"No. What you are seeing is the need for frugality. I have some family letters that look like that," he said. "Paper was scarce back then. To save paper, sometimes they would fill the page horizontally, then they would turn it sideways and write vertically over the original writing. Eliza had a lot to say and wanted to save paper. Good luck on deciphering it."

She studied the diary closer. Words flowed from side-to-side, then up-and-down and finally circled the narrow margin. Eliza had written with either a quill or steel-tipped pen. Adding to the difficulty of deciphering it was the faded ink and occasional blotches. Reading Eliza's diary was not going to be an easy task.

"Thanks, Tom," she said. "I really appreciate the good work you've done on this. Now, let's get this beautiful piece of furniture back where it belongs."

They wrestled the desk into the truck without mishap and installed it in the original corner of the keeper's office. All three stood back to admire their handiwork after it was finished.

"I wonder where old Liam learned to make something like this?" Jack said.

"Katherine told me he worked as a ship's carpenter before he married Eliza." Moriah glanced down at the diary she held. "I can't wait to read this. I have a feeling it is going to answer a lot of questions."

Jack plucked it out of her hands. "You need to wait until we get the tower finished."

"Please give that back," she said.

"I'm serious." Jack held it out of her reach. "I know how obsessed you've always been about Eliza and this place. If you start trying to read this now, we won't see you again for days. Or if you do come out to the worksite, you'll be all bleary-eyed from being up all night trying to read this handwriting. You need to leave it alone until winter."

Moriah made another attempt to get it back. Jack tossed the diary to Luke. "Here," he said. "Go hide this in a safe place."

"Don't you dare!"

Luke glanced between her and Jack. Then he made his decision and trotted outside with Eliza's diary in his hand.

"It's for your own good," Jack said. "You only have a few more evenings with Crystal before she has to leave. Now is the time for you to concentrate. I'll give the diary back to you after Crystal is gone and after our lighthouse project is finished."

Jack was right. She did need to focus and the diary would be a major distraction.

"You know me well, my friend," she said.

Chapter Twelve

For the next few days, she haunted the Little Current bridge. The people who lived nearby grew used to the sight of her taking a few steps, backing off, taking a few more, and backing off.

Crossing the bridge was complicated in that it swung out over the river every hour on the hour to give tall boats a chance to continue on their way through the North Channel. She did not want to even think about getting trapped on the bridge while it swung out.

Hourly she crept farther, inch-by-inch, marking her progress with chalk, never allowing herself to force her way too far past the line that would send her into a panic attack. It was exhausting work—the hardest she had ever done.

"I'm not sure you can undo twenty years in a week," Crystal said, during one of her trips to check on Moriah.

"Are you and your family enjoying your vacation?" Moriah asked.

"Yes."

"Do you need anything?"

"No."

"Then, I have work to do here, Crystal."

"Yes, you do," Crystal said. "I'll let you get back to it."

But no matter how hard Moriah tried, she could not go past the halfway point. It was as though an invisible, impenetrable wall separated her from the remaining half of the bridge.

She was trying to figure out what else to do, when Sam Black Hawk trotted up, his long, gray braids bouncing behind him as he ran. He wore black running shorts, new running shoes, a red bandana tied around his head and a green t-shirt emblazoned with the words: "KISS ME! I'm A Herpetologist."

"You manage to cross it yet?" He jogged in place.

"No, not yet. How did you know what I'm trying to do?"

"Half the island knows what you're trying to do, child." He stopped jogging, checked his pulse and sat down on the bench beside her. "What we don't know is if you're going to do it."

"Half the island knows?"

"Probably. We got a bet going on over at the reservation. Some think you'll win. Some figure the bridge will beat you."

"What are the odds?"

"About two-to-one last I heard."

"In my favor?"

"No."

The sack lunch Moriah had packed sat unopened on the bench between them. Black Hawk noticed, investigated, and helped himself to a bag of chips and a water bottle.

"I hear you talked a therapist into coming to the resort."

"How do you *know* all these things?"

"Smoke signals." He reached into her lunch bag again and discovered the peanut butter and jelly sandwich she'd packed. "Do you want half of this?"

She didn't know whether to be miffed or amused by the old man. Since he'd rid Cabin One of snakes, she chose to be amused. "You don't mind sharing?"

"No, I don't mind." He handed her half and took a bite out of the remaining half. "Needs more jelly."

"I'll try to remember that."

Black Hawk munched a bite of his sandwich with a faraway look in his eyes.

"Do you ever get angry, Moriah?"

"I try not to. Why?"

He took a swig out of her only water bottle. "Ahh! Nothing like a water after a five-mile run."

"Five miles?"

"Yeah. I got five still to go before I can call it a day."

"How *old* are you, anyway, Sam?"

"Old enough to know the power of anger."

"I don't understand."

"Anger can be a powerful tool when used correctly," Black Hawk said. "It can give you the strength to do what you need to do. Truth be told, I've been ashamed of you this summer."

"You barely know me," she said. "Why would you be ashamed of me?"

"All that sitting around whining and complaining you've been doing."

"I haven't been whining and complaining."

"You're doing it right now." He made his voice into a falsetto. "Poor little Moriah Robertson. Too weak and scared to walk across the bridge. Afraid she might get a bellyache or feel a little dizzy."

Anger flickered within her. "That's not fair."

"Then fight *harder!*" His voice grew strong, and he hit the bench between them with his fist. "You've got Ojibwe blood running through your veins, child. It's time you started acting like it! Our people have endured many things, but we have never been cowards."

"You don't understand." The flicker caught and her anger flared up. "I might have some issues, but I'm *not* a coward."

"Sure you are. You're sitting here thinking you don't have to overcome this. You're thinking Ben will come back and marry you anyway. Maybe you're right. The man did strike me as a bit foolish."

"What makes you think you're such an expert on my life?" Moriah said, hurt. "And don't tell me smoke signals."

"I'm a long distance runner. I hear things. I see things. I talk to people," Black Hawk said. "Ben's a linguist. He needs to be able to travel. How long do you think a marriage will last that's built on defeat? How long do you think it will take him to start resenting you?"

"Ben would never resent me."

"Possibly. But you can bet your bottom dollar Ben doesn't want to be married to a coward. What if one of your kids or Ben gets sick or bad hurt? What do you plan to do? Curl up and have a panic attack while you wait for someone else to show up and take over? You think Ben could forgive you if you lost a child because you were too scared to drive across the bridge to the hospital?

The old man was right and, for reasons she didn't entirely understand, the truth of what he was saying made her furious. Her anger had been building as he spoke. Anger at him for lecturing her. Anger at being forced into this situation. Anger at herself for not being able to overcome it.

The bridge swung back to allow the line of traffic to cross.

Black Hawk closed his eyes and began to sing in a soft, wailing, rhythmic chant as he ignored her and everything else around him. The words were not understandable, but the sound filled her heart with courage. She was a Robertson, but she was more than a Robertson. She did have First Nation blood running in her veins. Her people had never been cowards.

She picked up the chalk she had been using to mark her steps, rose from the bench and approached the bridge. As she drew nearer, the anger increased. This time, she did not try to shut it down but allowed it to grow and fill her body. Her brain swelled with it until she felt like her mind was on fire.

Behind her, Black Hawk's chant grew louder, then blended in with all the other background noise of the traffic and wind. Her fury grew until the only thing she heard was her own pulse pounding too loudly in her ears.

She had heard people use the term "seeing red" when they were angry and she had thought it was just an expression. Now, she discovered that it was not. The anger she felt was so extreme, her eyes literally saw red.

As she stepped onto the bridge, she tossed the chalk aside. It was unnecessary and bothersome.

A tour bus drove through, rattling the bridge, and Moriah didn't stop. A carload of teenagers drove by with music thundering out of their car, and she didn't stop. A heavy garbage truck lumbered through, rattling the bridge with its ponderous weight. She barely noticed.

It was at the halfway point when her stomach rebelled. She paused, breathed deeply, got the nausea under control, then with a loud cry she pushed her way past the halfway barrier—head down, butting her way through like an enraged bull. Twenty years of pain and anger flared hot and bright, fueling every step.

Through the bridge's groans and snaps, through the sound of rushing water beneath her, the caw of seagulls circling above her, Moriah crossed the length of the bridge, stepped down onto non-Manitoulin soil, scooped up a handful of dirt, and carried it triumphantly back across the bridge before the anger could wane.

"Here." She dumped the soil into Black Hawk's hand. "I did it."

Sam pulled the bandana he'd wrapped around his head, and reverently wrapped the dirt in it.

"It's just dirt, Sam." Moriah stood over him, still panting from the effort she'd expended.

"Just dirt? I disagree," Black Hawk said. "It was bought at too steep of a price."

Hands on hips, chin up, chest heaving, Moriah gazed at the bridge she had finally conquered.

"You'll need to do that again tomorrow, and the day after that, and the day after that," Black Hawk said. "Until it becomes commonplace. It's like the conditioning involved in running. You can't just walk away and forget it for a while or your legs start to get all rubbery."

Moriah nodded. "Got it."

Sam stood and gripped Moriah's shoulder. "I'm proud of you, daughter."

"Thank you." Moriah laid her hand over Black Hawk's as he grasped her shoulder. She had done it. She had left Manitoulin soil and the sky hadn't fallen.

"Thank you, Sam."

"You need to keep this." He chuckled a bit as he handed her the dirt-filled bandana tied with a knot.

"What are you laughing at?" She carefully tucked the bandana into her pants pocket.

"I'm not laughing at anything, child. That's sheer happiness you're hearing. I just won two-hundred dollars."

"How?"

"Two-to-one odds."

"You placed a hundred dollar bet on me?" She didn't know whether to be hurt or grateful. At least he hadn't bet against her.

"What are you talking about?" He acted shocked. "I don't gamble."

"Then what…?"

"I don't gamble. It was a sure thing."

"How could you have been so sure?"

"Easy. A woman with the nerve to keep herself under control while trapped beneath a cabin with a mess of rattlesnakes... well, I knew it was just a matter of time before you crossed the bridge. Did my song help?"

"It did. What was it? Another achy breaky heart song you made up?"

"Ben told you about that, did he?"

"He did."

"No. That was the real thing—an Ojibwe war song—because as far as I could see, it was high time you went to war."

He held out the half-full bottle of water. "You want the rest of this?"

"You can have it."

"Great." He drained it. Threw the empty bottle into a nearby trashcan, and jogged away.

"Where are you going?" she called.

"Got two hundred dollars to collect!"

The bridge swung out into the water, boats slipped through the narrow channel and then the bridge swung back. Moriah approached the bridge again. This time she would succeed because now she knew she could. Besides that, she was still angry, and she suspected she had been angry for a long time. She just hadn't realized it until today.

Chapter Thirteen

By the time Moriah drove all the way back from Little Current, the lights were out in Crystal's cabin. That was a disappointment because she badly wanted to tell her friend what she had accomplished that day. Instead of risking waking the children, she placed Black Hawk's bandana on the porch and left a note beneath it saying, "This contains *four* handfuls of dirt from Goat Island. Now, I am free!"

When she got back to the lodge, her desire to tell Ben what she had accomplished was so great that she pulled out an old spiral-bound notebook, curled up on the couch and wrote her heart out to him. She told him about how well Alicia was doing in helping her run the place, how great Jack was getting along, how beautiful the completed foghorn room was. She told him about the desk, and the surprise of Tom finding the contents of the hidden drawer, as well as the fact that baby Betsy had gotten two new baby teeth.

She saved the best news for last. Toward the end, she told him about how she had been able to thrust herself past the halfway point on the bridge. She told him about the dirt she had brought back from the other side. She described Sam Black Hawk's part in it all. Then she told him how much she loved and missed him.

That night she slept more soundly than she could ever remember sleeping in her life. No dreams. No nightmares. No waking in the middle of the night to check the clock to see if it was time to get up yet.

Normally, she did not set an alarm clock because it was her habit to awaken as soon as the sun rose. Today, it was nearly eight o'clock. Crystal and her family had planned to leave around noon today, so she intended to head over there as soon as she got dressed.

But when she went down to the kitchen, she found a note sitting beneath a small, clear, jar with a gold, metallic lid. The note was from Crystal, thanking her for her hospitality and saying that they'd had to leave early. Something about a children's birthday party back in Cleveland. The note included Crystal's office phone number, home phone number and cell phone.

Moriah felt a stab of disappointment. She had hoped to celebrate in some small way with the woman who had become such a friend to her.

The clear jar looked like it had once housed a decorative candle. The candle was gone and, in the bottom of the jar, lay the four handfuls of earth she'd left on the porch. Beside it was Black Hawk's red bandana, neatly folded.

Taped on the side of the jar were words written in Crystal's precise handwriting.

"Don't stop. Fill this jar to the top. Don't let the giants win!"

"I won't, my friend," Moriah whispered.

She grabbed the jar and strode out to the truck. There was a great deal to do today. Jack and the men would be working on the wooden flooring in the light tower and there was a need for more lumber. She wanted to clean Number Ten cabin now that Crystal and her family had left. Guests from Toronto were scheduled to arrive this evening. The day was absolutely packed.

But first, she had a bridge to cross again. She needed to fill the candle jar with more dirt from Goat Island.

Chapter Fourteen

....

Ben stood at the top of a high gorge looking at a rope bridge with short, wooden planks laid across it. The spray from a nearby waterfall kept the planks wet and slippery. His good friend, Rashawe, stood beside him.

"So this is where it happened?" Ben asked, in Yahnowa.

"Yes," Rashawe replied, in his native tongue. "This is where my father almost fell while carrying the child."

"What saved him?"

"I heard his cry, turned, and held out my spear. It was just enough to steady him."

"Was he angry at Moriah?"

"He was more frightened than angry, but he shouted at her. I'm sure he sounded angry to her. Do you want to cross it now?"

"No," Ben said. "I can't imagine *anyone* actually *wanting* to cross it."

"It is probably sturdier now than the day we walked it with Little Green Eyes."

Ben eyed it suspiciously. "When is the last time anyone used it?"

In answer, Rashawe stepped onto the bridge and easily walked across it. When he arrived at the other side, he called back. "This is the last time anyone used it."

Rashawe and Ben had become good friends these past five years. They were about the same age and Rashawe was quick to learn. Ben was fairly certain he would someday take his father's place as leader of the

Yahnowa tribe. He would make an excellent leader. Rashawe was also making headway in learning English. He loved his people and had a calm, strong spirit. He also had a sense of humor—like right now—grinning at Ben from the other side of the gorge. It was a dare, if Ben had ever seen one.

Actually, Ben had intended to walk this bridge anyway, as long as it looked sturdy enough. He had not intended for Rashawe to test the bridge for him—but it did convince him that the bridge would hold his weight. Ben grabbed hold of the two ropes that acted as handrails, and took his first careful step onto the bridge that had terrified Moriah as a child.

He did not have to do this, of course. It wouldn't have anything to do with whether or not Moriah overcame her fears, but he missed her so badly. Walking this bridge that, according to Rashawe, had not changed much since she'd been carried across it, was a way to feel closer to her. When he saw her again, he would be able to tell her that he'd crossed it and could understand why it had been so scary.

Well, actually, he didn't have to cross it to see why it had been so scary. It was a *long* way to the bottom of the gorge, and the gorge was wide. It took a lot of trust in one's fellow man's ability to construct something sturdy out of wood and homemade rope to venture onto it.

Rashawe was squatting at the end of it now, making encouraging motions for him to cross.

The wooden slat beneath his feet creaked, and the rope made a slight groaning noise as he stepped on and allowed his full weight to be supported entirely by the bridge. He waited a moment to get his bearings and balance, then took another step. Even though there were ropes attached at waist level on both sides to use as handrails, it still took a good bit of balance to walk across the narrow bridge. It felt as though it wouldn't take much for it to twist in midair and leave him hanging from it upside down.

There was a fine spray that wafted in on the currents of wind stirred from the waterfall and it made the wooden slats slick with moisture. He felt his right foot slip, but caught himself. The waterfall was lovely, but the beauty of nature was not particularly important to him right now. Getting safely across the bridge was.

Ben took four more steps, feeling the bridge sway with each one. He glanced down again. It was incredibly far to the bottom. The thought that it might be wise to carry a parachute with him if he ever did this again, skittered across his mind.

Then it happened. He was focusing on the depth of the gorge and forgot to step carefully. His right foot slipped again, this time sideways out from under him, and his leg went over the edge. The foot bridge tipped precariously, causing his entire body to shift and then slide off.

Suddenly he was dangling in mid-air, his feet pedaling desperately. The only thing keeping him from falling to the bottom of the gorge was his death grip on the rope handrail.

As he tried to kick and maneuver his way into a better position, he was grateful for the muscle he had built these past weeks of hefting stone. He was as strong as he had ever been.

"Hold on!" Rashawe called. "I'm coming."

Ben continued to hang in midair as Rashawe worked his way over to him. He felt the bridge shift as Rashawe righted it with his own weight, and then laid down on his stomach and reached a strong arm down to grasp Ben's. He held on to Ben and counterbalanced the bridge with his own body while Ben clawed his way back up. Their faces were inches apart as Ben flopped flat onto his belly, trying to catch his breath and stop shaking after such a close call.

Moriah's horrific memory was accurate. It was very possible for someone to fall off the bridge.

"I don't understand," Ben said. "Why were you able to go across so easily?"

Rashawe carefully sat back on his haunches and lifted one calloused bare foot for Ben to inspect. "Much better for crossing a wet bridge than your white man's shoes."

"Obviously," Ben said.

"I'm guessing you want to go back?" Rashawe said.

"Oh, yeah." Ben struggled to a half-crouch, found his balance, stood up and very carefully faced the way he'd come. "I don't need to go the rest of the way to understand why Moriah has a problem with crossing bridges."

Chapter Fifteen

Moriah was surprised when Katherine and Nicolas walked through the front door of the lodge a day sooner than she expected. Alicia had not yet come in for the day and Moriah was busy doing laundry before heading out to the worksite.

"You're back." Moriah was carrying a basket of freshly laundered towels. She sat the towels on the couch as Katherine rushed to hug her.

"It is so good to see you, Moriah!"

Moriah hugged her back, but she had mixed feelings about Katherine right now. For one thing, there was the issue of the hidden photos to be dealt with. She had carefully replaced them in Katherine's bottom drawer. After she and Nicolas settled in, she intended to approach her about it.

"Did you have a good time?"

"We had a *wonderful* time," Katherine whirled around with her arms outstretched while Nicolas looked on, adoringly. "But it feels good to be home."

Moriah picked up the basket of towels and settled them against her hip while she took a good look at Katherine. Her aunt had changed. She looked ten years younger than at the beginning of the summer, and she was glowing with happiness. The dress she wore, a pastel, floral dress, was made from some sort of floaty material. It was something she would never have worn before Nicolas showed up.

She had also cut off her braids for the first time in Moriah's memory, and her hair had magically lost its threads of gray. It had been styled into a shoulder length cut that perfectly framed her face.

The change was unsettling.

"You colored and cut your hair."

"I know it's a tremendous change," Katherine glanced back at her new husband and smiled. "But Nicolas likes it."

"It looks nice."

Katherine had been gray even in her late twenties. Moriah had never seen her aunt without long, salt-and-pepper braids.

Katherine self-consciously reached up a hand to pat her hair and Moriah got her second surprise.

"You have palm trees painted on your fingernails!"

Katherine looked at her fingernails as though just discovering them. "It seemed like fun at the time." There was a hint of apology in her voice. "I think I'll go change now. It's been a long trip."

Moriah stared as her aunt climbed the stairs, her pretty skirt swirling around her knees, sandals decorated with fake gemstones glittering on her feet. The transformation was immense. Who *was* this woman with whom she had shared the past twenty years of her life?

She shook her head and turned away, stepping right into the glare of Nicolas who, unless she was mistaken, was furious.

"How dare you!" Nicolas said.

"What?" Moriah was defensive.

"Do you realize how hard I had to work to talk Katherine into making those changes?"

"If you love her, why change her?"

Nicolas wiped a hand over his face, as though trying to wipe away the anger. When he replied, his voice was measured.

"I would love Katherine in buckskin and beads, in sackcloth and ashes, with hair down to her ankles, or in a buzz cut. But what I *remember* is a beautiful, happy girl who curled her hair and wore ribbons in it. I remember what she was like before she became a slave to this resort and to you."

"That's not fair."

"You didn't ask for her to sacrifice for you." Nicolas's voice was weary. "That was Katherine's choice. But you are no longer a child, Moriah. It's time for your aunt to have her own life; to feel young. She's only in her forties and *look* at her, she's gorgeous and she's happy."

Moriah heard steps on the stairwell, glanced up, and her heart dropped. Katherine had changed into an old, drab, housedress. She had pulled her hair back off her face and washed off her bit of makeup.

"Either of you want coffee?" Katherine said. "I'll make some."

"Nothing for me," Moriah said. "I need to drop these towels off at cabin three, then meet the electrician who is coming to install outlets in the lantern room."

"Looks like you've made a lot of progress since we've been gone," Nicolas said. "I'll be out later to see what you and Ben accomplished before he had to leave."

Her emotions were in a jumble as she left. She was still upset with Katherine over the photos, but she'd missed her terribly. Now her aunt was back—but was no longer the same person. The Katherine she had known would have been aghast if someone had tried to decorate her fingernails with palm trees. But Nicolas was right. Katherine was gorgeous and very happy.

She dropped off the towels and finished making up the beds in cabin three, then she drove toward the worksite.

Nicolas' comment about her fear of change was unfair and had hurt. The thing that hurt most was that Nicolas was right. She liked the safety of routine. She hated change. Hated the idea of Katherine being different. Change, in her life, had always meant loss. It was probably the real reason behind her dislike for Nicolas. He had managed to initiate three cataclysmic changes in her life. The appearance of Ben, the loss of the lighthouse and Katherine getting married.

Even though she was upset with her aunt for keeping the knowledge of her parent's death a secret and hiding the photos of them, she still loved her. Everyone was flawed. Everyone had secrets. Katherine probably less than most.

Her aunt had been so happy and young-looking when she entered the lodge, so filled with life. And Moriah had ruined it all with a few comments.

She swung the truck around and headed to Little Current. Jack would be fine without her for another hour or so. She wanted to go across the bridge one more time. This time she intended to *drive* over it.

She felt fairly secure in trying this. By now she had crossed it so many times on foot that she had an intimate knowledge of it. Knew exactly how many steel plates were welded together to make the pedestrian sidewalk. Had counted the rivets in those steel plates. Knew every sound, every clank, every shimmer. It was still a black, metal giant, but a benevolent giant. Her giant. She had conquered it and she owned it now.

Once she knew for certain she could drive over it, she intended to give Katherine a big surprise—a surprise that might cancel out the disapproval she had heard today in her own voice.

Chapter Sixteen

When she arrived at the bridge, she entered it without feeling the least bit nervous. Ben would be so proud of her calm.

She could already visualize herself on the other side, grabbing another fistful of dirt to add to the jar Crystal had given her.

She drove with her right hand on the steering wheel, and her left elbow nonchalantly hanging out of the open window. She could feel the wind in her hair. No qualms. No lurching stomach. No heart palpitations.

Nearly halfway across, she heard a crash. The car in front of her came to an abrupt stop and Moriah stomped on her brakes so suddenly, her truck engine died. The car behind her missed ramming her bumper by inches.

The driver of the car behind her laid on his horn. She turned to look at him. Probably an impatient tourist. An islander wouldn't act that way. Couldn't he see something was wrong up ahead?

She pushed herself out her window and sat on the edge, straining to look over the cars in front. As she had suspected, there was a wreck up ahead. People were already piling out of their cars to investigate.

She glanced back, again, at the man in the car behind her. He was gesturing oddly and continuing to honk his horn—as though *she* could do anything about the wreck!

Then it struck her where she was. She couldn't go forward. She couldn't go backward. She was pinned in on all sides, here on this bridge.

Trapped.

Her mouth grew dry and she felt dizzy. She slipped back down into the driver's seat before she could fall out. Not a panic attack! Not now when she had been doing so well...

Honk! Honk!

Why did this idiot keep honking his horn at her?

Her panic attack was suddenly replaced with annoyance. She grabbed the truck handle, opened the door, slid out and walked back to the car. Her legs were a bit wobbly but, otherwise, she was pretty steady.

"So, what's your problem?" She approached the man's window. "There's been an accident up ahead. I can't move my truck, no matter how much you honk."

"Chest pains." The man was elderly and he was pale and shaking.

"I'll get help!" Moriah was off like a shot. She flew to the front of the bridge where a large knot of people had gathered around two damaged cars.

"There's a man having a heart attack back there," she shouted. "I need an ambulance."

"One's already coming." A young man said. He was holding one of those bulky car phones. "We called as soon as we saw the crash, but it's not as bad as we thought."

Two people had been helped out of the wrecked cars. Neither seemed to be badly hurt, although the back of one of their cars was crushed and the front of the one behind was crumpled. A siren sounded nearby.

"Send the EMTs to the blue Lincoln," she instructed. "Tell them to hurry!"

She raced back to the old man and found him breathing raggedly and clutching his chest.

"Hang on, the ambulance is on its way. They'll be here any second now."

"Bless you," the man gasped.

Two EMTs hurried toward them, pushing a gurney. They checked him over quickly. Then they helped him out of the car, buckled him onto the collapsible gurney and wheeled him to the ambulance.

As the siren ebbed away, the car in front of her began to move. The young man with the car phone who had called for the ambulance made his way toward her.

"We've pushed the wreck out of the way," he said. "People can drive around it. Cops are talking to the ones involved. If you think it's okay, I'll drive the old man's car off the bridge and park it."

"Someone needs to," Moriah said. "Thanks."

She drove off the bridge and pulled into the small parking lot on the other side. The police were indeed questioning some people and were inspecting the two wrecked vehicles. She watched as the old man's car was parked, and the young man handed the keys over to the police. She waited there until everyone, including the cops, cleared out. As she watched, the bridge slowly began its rotation out over the water again as several boats went through.

She had been trapped on it. Trapped and starting to panic. Then she had responded to the old man's suffering and forgotten that she was afraid. Funny how thinking about someone besides herself had made the panic go away.

Getting back out of the truck, she squatted in the gravel and brushed it aside until she could scoop up another small handful of dirt. The jar that Crystal had given her sat on the ground beside her. She let the handful sift through her fingers into it. She had pretended to herself that, when she'd managed to fill the jar with hard-earned dirt from the other side of the bridge, she would be well. The handful didn't completely fill it. There was still an inch of space left.

It didn't matter.

She already knew she was going to be okay.

Chapter Seventeen

Moriah didn't expect to see Katherine fixing supper when she got home from meeting the electrician who was going to be installing outlets.

"I'm sorry," Moriah lifted the lid on a pot and investigated. "I would have had something ready for you and Nicolas if I'd known you were coming home today."

"It wasn't any trouble. I missed my kitchen," Katherine said. "Besides, Alicia peeled potatoes and fried the chicken while I held little Betsy. That sweet baby grew so much while we were away."

Moriah snagged a piece of celery off a vegetable tray. "It's good to have you…"

Suddenly, she noticed that the two photo albums belonging to her parents were lying on the counter—the ones she had found in Katherine's bottom drawer.

Her aunt was busy tearing up lettuce for a salad.

"What's that?" Moriah said.

"What's what?" Katherine asked, preoccupied.

"The two photo albums on the counter."

"Oh," Katherine glanced over her shoulder. "Those are for you. I put those albums away when you were little because I was afraid, if you saw those pictures, it would trigger yet something else that your grandfather and I would not know how to deal with. I'm afraid I spent most of your young years walking on egg shells, trying to protect you from any more pain."

"Why are you bringing them out now?" Moriah asked.

Katherine looked perplexed at her question. "Because you should have them, of course. I'd almost forgotten about them. Then, on our trip, Nicolas was taking a picture of me and suddenly I remembered. Maybe we can look through them together sometime. There's probably questions you might have that I can answer."

Her aunt's explanation was so reasonable that Moriah's suspicion and worry about Katherine's motives simply drained away. Wordlessly, she walked over, put her arms around Katherine's waist and hugged her.

"My hands are still wet from rinsing the salad." Katherine held her hands out away from Moriah. "I'll get water on you."

"I don't care," Moriah said.

Katherine returned her hug in spite of damp hands. "Supper will be ready in fifteen minutes."

Moriah's heart was light as she went up the stairs to her room to change out of her work clothes. Her feelings about Katherine were back to normal. Questions answered. Reasonable explanations given. She could feel her trust returning.

As she walked past Katherine's room, she noticed the door was open and Nicolas was sound asleep on Katherine's bed. That felt a little weird, but she shrugged it off. If being married to Nicolas made her aunt happy it was fine with her.

Chapter Eighteen

"Anything interesting happen while we were gone?" Nicolas asked, as they sat down to the fried chicken supper Katherine had helped prepare. He seemed determined to be civil, but his annoyance about her less-than-positive reaction to the changes in Katherine that morning tinged his voice. "Any hiccoughs with the restoration?"

"No problems, but we did have one big surprise."

"And what was that, dear." Katherine sat a basket of paper napkins on the table.

"Do you remember how we removed the big desk that was in the keeper's office?"

"Yes," Nicolas said. "If I remember right, you took it to a man on the island who refinishes furniture."

"Tom Hawkins," Moriah said. "He does really good work. Something like seven layers of varnish and he sands in-between each layer. It takes him forever to finish a piece, but he's worth waiting for."

"So you're pleased?" Katherine said.

"More than pleased. Tom discovered a small, secret drawer."

"Really?" Katherine said. "I grew up with that desk and no one ever said anything about a secret drawer."

"Maybe they didn't know."

"So... don't keep us in suspense." Nicolas smiled. "Did you find the treasure map to the famed Robertson fortune?"

"You mean the nonexistent Robertson fortune?" Moriah said. "No, it was Eliza Robertson's diary."

"You can't be serious!" Katherine said. "Have you read it?"

"No," Moriah said. "Jack took it away from me."

"Why would Jack do something like that?" Nicolas asked.

"He said I would get too involved, stay up all night, and come to the worksite groggy from lack of sleep. He said I can only get it back after the lighthouse is finished and we've had our open house."

"One wonders," Nicolas said. "Who's the boss out at the job site? You or Jack?"

"Moriah is the boss, but Jack knows her well," Katherine said. "He's right. She wouldn't have been able to put it down."

"I suppose I could go to Jack and insist he turn it over to me," Nicolas said. "I'm curious too."

"That wouldn't be fair, dear," Katherine said. "Moriah should get to be the first one who reads it. She is the one who cares the most."

"Oh, okay," Nicolas grumbled. "But I lived in that lighthouse too, remember?"

"Oh, I remember." Katherine briefly covered his hand with her own. "I remember well."

A look passed between them that Moriah envied.

"So," Nicolas said, when they stopped gazing at each other and Katherine passed him the mashed potatoes. "Did you and Jack make any progress today?"

"Some. You should go see it."

"Kathy and I'll go over tomorrow morning." He lifted a crisp chicken leg onto his plate. "It's getting late."

"Actually, I had plans for Katherine tomorrow if you don't mind." Moriah savored the moment.

"Oh?" Katherine glanced up at her.

"It's a Saturday. I thought we might go shopping." Moriah nonchalantly ladled potatoes onto her plate.

"Shopping? For what?" Katherine passed a bowl of peas.

"I need some nicer clothes." Moriah dipped peas onto her plate. "Something pretty—like what you were wearing this afternoon."

Nicolas stopped chewing, swallowed, put down his fork and watched her closely. Moriah could almost feel him daring her to say something that would embarrass Katherine.

"Where did you want to go? There isn't a very big selection here on the island," Katherine said. "You know that."

"Oh! I forgot to show you something. Would you excuse me a moment?" Moriah rose.

Katherine and Nicolas glanced at each other as she left the table as though wondering what was going on. She couldn't wait to see the expression in their eyes when she told them.

After returning to the kitchen with Crystal's jar in her hand, she placed it in the center of the table, resumed her seat and began eating again without uttering a word.

"And that is?" Nicolas lifted the jar and shook it.

"Dirt."

"Dirt?"

"Yes." She spread butter on a piece of bread. "Dirt."

"Is there something particularly special about it?" Katherine asked.

"Nope. Nothing special at all. It's just common old Canadian dirt."

"As lovely as it is," Nicolas said, "why are you using it as a centerpiece for our table?"

"It's dirt I picked up from Goat Island after I crossed the bridge." Moriah lifted her chin and met Katherine's eyes, allowing her pride and happiness to shine through. "I thought maybe Katherine would like to go to the mall in Espanola with me tomorrow. I'll drive."

"Goat Island?" Katherine said. "You didn't!"

"Oh yes, ma'am, I did!"

"If you're joking about this…" Nicolas' voice was filled with warning.

"It's not a joke. I *did* it!" Both of Moriah's fists hit the table. She felt so proud. "Over and over and over again. I *crossed* it!"

"How?" Katherine's voice was filled with wonder.

"I found out about a really good therapist while the two of you were away. I gave her and her family a free, two-week vacation here at the resort while she worked with me."

"I considered importing a specialist," Nicolas mused. "But I didn't think you would accept it."

"I wouldn't have." Moriah said. "It was something I had to do for myself."

"All these years," Katherine said. "I kept hoping…"

"So," Moriah held her truck keys out and jingled them, "want to go shopping tomorrow?"

Chapter Nineteen

....

Moriah lay awake long into the night after their Saturday excursion. It had felt so good to finally go shopping at the mall like normal people. She was exhausted, but too excited to settle down. The day had felt extraordinary.

First, they went to the hospital to check on the old man who had survived having a heart attack on the bridge. He was doing well. His daughter expressed her thanks to Moriah for helping him.

Then she and Katherine explored the mall together for the first time in her life. Nicolas insisted on being their chauffeur and seemed pleased by their excitement. The man had his moments.

Best of all, she had taken a quick peek at wedding dresses! Not serious shopping. She didn't try anything on. She was just daydreaming, but that was why she couldn't get calmed down enough to sleep. The world had begun to open up to her. So many possibilities once one was no longer bound by fear.

Giving up on sleep, she climbed out of bed and threw on her old bathrobe. Maybe a glass of milk would help.

Before she went out the door, she happily gave the globe another spin. This time her finger ended up on Greenland. She'd heard good things about its rugged beauty. Maybe she would go there someday. Only this time it wasn't a pipedream. There was a good possibility that soon, if she wanted to go to Greenland, she really could! The thought was exhilarating.

She trotted down the stairs after that glass of milk. Some crackers to go with it sounded good. Loading up on carbs always made her sleepy. They had church to go to in the morning and she needed to get some rest if she was going to keep from dozing during the preacher's sermon.

Nicolas was in the living room when she reached the main floor. In the past that would have annoyed her, but tonight it felt right having him here. She had definitely not enjoyed living in the lodge by herself these past weeks. Knowing that he and Katherine were here made her feel a lot better.

He was sitting at an old desk, working on his laptop computer.

He turned when he heard her.

"I'm glad you're awake, Moriah. I have something to show you."

She went and peered over his shoulder.

"While Kathy and I were in the Caymans, Ben contacted me. He told me that he'd had to leave Manitoulin, and why. When I heard that he was going back into the jungle, I planned for a solar-powered, satel-lite laptop computer to be taken in to him. I couldn't be entirely sure if it would be delivered, but it looks like he's received it and has figured out how to use it."

"Ben is smart."

"Yes, he is." Nicolas removed his glasses and got to his feet, offering her his chair. "I think you might be interested in this."

Moriah sat down, transfixed by her first introduction to a com-puter. Nicolas had already suggested that she and Katherine could run a smoother establishment with the help of one but, as always, Moriah disliked the idea of change and had balked.

She read the script eagerly.

Dear Nicolas,

Ron Meacham brought this computer last week. Fortunately, the clearing that the Yahnowa made so that Violet could be flown out, was still viable enough for him to set the old Huey down again. It is a testament to their love for her that Abraham could convince them to create that clearing at all. The Yahnowa are not fond of making access to their village convenient, and I can't blame them. Ron has gotten word that Violet is not doing well, even though she is back in the states. I pray for a recovery but I'm afraid it might be too late unless God grants a miracle.

Speaking of miracles. This laptop is only a little short of one. Thank you for sending it. I'd considered getting one at the end of the summer, but, as you now know, there wasn't time. It took me awhile to figure out how everything works on it, but what a blessing!

With the Smiths gone, my life here seems especially strange. They always softened the culture shock when I came back before.

I miss Manitoulin, I miss working on the lighthouse but, most of all, I miss Moriah. If you get this, please give her my love and tell her I'm okay.

Ben

Moriah whirled around and found Nicolas standing behind her, waiting for her reaction.

"You are a kind man," she said, with wonder. "Thank you!"

"You've decided to like me now?" He smiled. "If only I'd known all it would take was a satellite laptop..."

Moriah propelled herself off the chair and hugged his neck.

"You did this so Ben and I could talk to each other!"

"Yes, I did." Nicolas hugged her back, awkwardly. "If you're happy, Kathy is happy. If Kathy is happy..."

Moriah dropped back into the seat before he could finish.

"Show me how to work this thing!"

After a quick session, Nicolas went to bed, giving her the privacy to communicate with Ben alone. Laboriously, she hunted for keys and pecked out her news. Typing had never become part of her skillset.

dear ben,

i crossed the bridge today. it wasn't my first time, either.

me and katherine went shopping in espanola. we even kind of looked at wedding dresses. when i can fly without freaking out we can get married if you still want to.

i love you

moriah

Dear Moriah,

YOU CROSSED THE BRIDGE??? I know men aren't supposed to cry, but I'm bawling right now from gratitude and relief. Of course, I still want us to get married. Your strength amazes me. Yesterday Rashawe took me to the rope bridge that his father carried you across on that terrible night our parents died. It's the one you nearly fell off. It was a long hike to go see it, but I'm glad I went there. I now can understand why bridges have been difficult for you. That gorge by the waterfall is terrifying even in daytime. I can hardly imagine what it was like for you as a child and in the dark.

Love,

Ben

Error

87

Chapter Twenty

Schools began to open as late August settled onto Manitoulin, and the guests at Robertson's Resort dwindled even more until the cabins were completely deserted. Moriah drained pipes and prepared the resort for winter. Katherine line-dried all the linens, and stored them in the laundry room on shelves that Moriah had built for that purpose. The linens were laced, for the first time, with sachets of dried lavender—something Katherine had learned from the resort in the Cayman's where she and Nicolas had honeymooned.

Together, along with Nicolas, they turned mattresses, made certain there wasn't a crumb of food in any of the cabins to interest mice, brought in the boats and turned them belly up to repel rain and snow.

Moriah checked each boat motor then tucked it snugly into a special bin inside the storage shed. In the past, these tasks had signaled the beginning of her least favorite season, when she and Katherine would sometimes be housebound for weeks while the snow piled up around their home. Neither Moriah nor Katherine were the kind of women who enjoyed sitting. They both went nearly stir-crazy by February every year.

This winter would probably be the same, except for one thing.

If Moriah had her way, she wouldn't be here.

It's warm here all the time, Moriah, and fragrant with the smell of flowers and rain. How I wish you could lie in my arms

at night and listen to the sounds of the jungle moving about us.
Love,
Ben

Dear Ben
Wish I took typing in school! Nicolas showed me how to make capital letters last night. I'm slow as molasses on this thing, and there is so much to say! Jack and me and the crew only have a few more days to be finished. The lighthouse looks real good. Bob Wilson Jr. says he'll take me up in his piper cub when I'm ready. Now that I've walked the bridge, I'm going out to the airport to look the plane over and take pictures of it so I can start getting used to it, too. When I can face flying without going into a meltdown, I'll come. I want to hear those jungle sounds with you.
Love,
Moriah

Dear Moriah,
I am so proud of you, my sweet warrior. You are the bravest woman I have ever known. I love you beyond words, beyond life, beyond anything or anyone on this earth.
Your husband-to-be,
Ben

Dear Ben,
I stayed in the piper cub for an hour yesterday. Bob Jr. drove it up and down the runway and I didn't puke but I wanted to.
Love,
Moriah

Dear Moriah McCain

(You need to get used to the sound of your new name, sweetheart. I can't wait to hear people call you that.)

It was touch-and-go here for a while. Abraham was right. There were problems brewing. I've done what I could and I think things have stabilized. There is peace again between the tribes. At least for now. I feel I could leave the Yahnowa long enough to come to Manitoulin and bring back my bride. Do you have any idea when you'll be ready to face the flight?

I've been thinking, if Nicolas doesn't mind, Robertson's Lighthouse would be my first choice for a wedding. After all, it was what brought us together. Perhaps we could have the wedding after dark? Maybe rig a beacon in the tower and put lights in all the windows?

I dream about our wedding and about being able to hold you in my arms again. I miss you so much, I have to struggle to concentrate and do my work. Hurry and conquer flying so I can have you beside me.

Your loving Ben

P.S. Keep driving up and down the runway in that plane!

Dear Ben,

I think I can rig a beacon in the tower alright. Easier than rigging myself up. ha ha. It feels funny trying on wedding dresses but they sure are pretty. I bought one today. I hope you like it.

Moriah McCain

Dear Mrs. McCain,

I can't wait for the moment I see you in that wedding dress!

You will make such a beautiful bride.

Are you also getting clothes and supplies together for the jungle? Abraham sent me a list of things Violet says you'll need. By the way, she's doing better. The surgeon thinks he got all the cancer. They're doing chemo now. She and Abraham are already talking about returning, although I think it might be too soon for them to even consider it. Maybe it's nothing more than their way of keeping hope alive. Tell Nicolas not to stop looking for someone with medical training who is willing to come. Lord knows, these people could use some help.

I can bandage a cut and hand out some antibiotics or aspirin, but that's about it.

Love,

Ben

Chapter Twenty-One

Dear Ben,

Alicia let me watch her teach her Sunday school class this morning. First and second grade. If I keep going into class with her I think I might be able to teach the Yahnowa children some Bible stories after I learn their language. I'll try real hard to be a good missionary wife.

Love,

Moriah

P.S. I was able to go up in Bob Jr.'s plane today for five whole minutes before I made him land. I took a bucket in case I got sick, but I didn't have to use it.

Ben's throat tightened, reading her e-mail. He hated the fact that she had to fight so hard to come live with him and wished he could make it easier for her.

"I'm finished," Fusiwe said.

Fusiwe was in his mid-twenties and had been apprenticed to the local native healer since his late teens. Violet, with her nurse training had also taught him what she could. Fusiwe was quick to absorb knowledge and had developed an aspiration to add Western medicine to his repertoire. He and his wife were already fairly fluent in spoken English, but Fusiwe also wanted to learn to read and write it.

For the past few nights, he had started coming to Ben's hut every evening to spend a bit of time working on whatever written English assignment Ben gave him. The young healer was barely at first-grade level yet in written English, but that would change. Ben had seldom seen anyone as determined to learn as this man.

Ben clicked off the satellite computer and shut the lid. It was time to look over his friend's work. Tonight they had progressed to the words 'cat' and 'dog', which Fusiwe had painstakingly copied over and over.

"Good job," Ben said. "You are gaining more English words every day."

"How is your woman?" Fusiwe asked. "Those words you read are from her?"

"Yes," Ben said. "She's doing well. Today she went up in a plane for a few minutes."

Fusiwe, who had seldom seen an airplane, let alone ridden in one, nodded sagely. "That is a good thing."

"I hope so. I would like to have her here with me. I miss her."

"My wife sometimes speaks of the days when Little Green Eyes was here. She has grown into a beautiful woman?"

"You have no idea," Ben said. "Beautiful, kind and capable."

"How soon will she come?"

"It might take a few months," Ben said. "She was only in the air today for five minutes before she panicked and the pilot had to set her down again. The trip here takes many hours. I'm certain she won't be ready to get on a commercial flight until she knows for certain she can withstand it without falling apart. At that point, I will go marry her and bring her back here to live with me."

"I will leave now," Fusiwe said. "When you talk with her, tell her that we look forward to seeing her."

"I will do that," Ben said.

"But I think it might be wise not to tell her about Moawa."

A look passed between them.

"You're right," Ben said. "I won't tell her about Moawa until after she arrives. I will explain things to her then."

"Good." Fusiwe left to go back to his own family's hut.

A mosquito landed on Ben's arm and he swatted it. It seemed that no matter how much bug spray he used, the dratted things wouldn't leave him alone. He had heard that insects were particularly drawn to redheads. He could certainly attest to the fact that, at least in his case, it was most definitely true.

Ben opened the computer again and began to type.

Dear Moriah,

You stayed in the air five whole minutes! I'm so happy and proud of you!

How are the newlyweds? Still blissfully happy?

Love,

Ben

Dear Ben,

Blissful? The love birds I live with are ridiculous. They are so happy even the air feels all sweet and sticky around them. ha. ha. Jack is working on the wood flooring of the cottage. I wish we had the Fresnel lens back, then all would be perfect. I don't know what Nicolas will do with the place now that he has moved into the lodge, but it is beautiful. We did a good job.

Love,

Moriah

The heavy humidity outside made his hut feel like a steam bath. He closed the laptop, pushed it aside and scooted his Bible and spiral notebook over in front of him on the makeshift desk. In spite of the computer's capabilities, he felt more secure working with paper and pencil when it came to his translation. Hard copy was a good thing. Besides, he seemed to think better with a pencil and paper in hand. He was grateful he'd left the rest of his work with Moriah. It would be safe with her.

He worked long into the night until the pages began to swim in front of his eyes and the Yahnowa words lost their meaning. He was used to exhaustion, having been pushing himself ever since his arrival. But this time felt a little different. He felt feverish and achy and was rapidly getting worse.

With the walls of the hut swirling around him, he stumbled to his pallet and fell face down.

Chapter Twenty-Two

Moriah put her tools away and locked the storage shed after finishing a plumbing job on Cabin Seven. Then she drove to the lighthouse. Everything was finished there except varnishing the newly-sanded wooden floors in the keeper's house. Jack was working on them today. She had picked out a honey-colored stain for the oak flooring and couldn't wait to see how it looked.

"Don't come in!" Jack shouted as she approached. "The stain isn't dry. I don't want your feet messing up the job I've done."

She stood at the open door and looked in. The room gleamed. The woodwork had been stripped, sanded, and stained the same honey-color maple as the floor. A buttery yellow covered the walls. Early autumn sunlight flooded through the new windows.

"It's beautiful," she said.

"Nice place for a wedding, eh?"

"A small one. I figure this room can only hold about twenty people. How long before we can put furniture in?"

"I'd give it a day or two. What furniture?"

"My grandmother and grandfather's things are stored in the attic of the lodge. Some of it is original from the beginning of the lighthouse."

"You planning on charging admission on the place, or what?"

"I'm not sure what Nicolas has planned for it. Now that he and Katherine are married and living at the lodge, he seems to have completely lost interest in it."

"Are they still acting like lovebirds?"

"Pretty much. Katherine seems very happy."

"And Nicolas?"

"Nicolas is… well, Nicolas. He's tightly wrapped, but he seems to have focused his life on being good to Katherine, so I'm not complaining."

"Seems a shame for him to stop practicing medicine."

"He hasn't," Moriah said. "He and Katherine are working together these days over at Wikwemikong. She talked him into it but he doesn't seem to mind as long as she's with him."

"We can use another doctor on the island."

"I agree."

"Have you decided on the date for your wedding yet?"

"It depends. I want to be absolutely certain I can fly for a long period of time without falling apart before we set a date."

"How's the flying going?"

"I was able stay in the air a little longer yesterday than the day before. I do pretty good as long as we're above Manitoulin, but whenever Bob Jr. tries to head out over the lake I start having a rough time."

"You'll beat it."

"I will eventually, but I'm grateful that Bob Jr. is a patient man."

"You sure you can stay away from us once you do leave?" Jack asked. "The Amazon is very far away. You're going to miss us."

"Of course I'll miss everyone but, if I can be with Ben, I'll be okay." Moriah smiled. "Besides, we've decided we'll come back each summer so I can help Katherine run the resort when the tourists come. Ben says for you to keep an ear open for stonemason jobs he could do next summer while I'm working at the resort."

"I'll do that. Shouldn't be hard. People around here are impressed with the way he put that tower back together."

Moriah watched as Jack gathered his tools together. "Alicia has been wonderful help this summer. You two still doing okay?"

"Absolutely. Having steady work has helped. It isn't good for a man to be cooped up in the house for too long without a job."

"Do you have anything lined up when this job is over?"

"Not yet. I've put some feelers out."

"I hope something comes up."

"I do too." Jack pounded the lid down on the remaining bucket of stain and opened his toolkit. "It's going to be hard to walk away from this place. I've enjoyed the company and the work. Felt like we accomplished something important."

"We did."

"In fact," Jack pulled a zip-locked bag out of the bottom of his toolkit and tossed it to her. "I think I can safely give this to you, now. You've earned it."

Inside the zip-lock bag was Eliza Robertson's leather diary.

"Thanks," Moriah said. "Did you read any of it? Do you know what it says?"

"Nah," Jack said. "Alicia and me tried to read some of it together one night. With all that spidery handwriting and the faded ink, we couldn't make out much. Better get a good magnifying glass before you attempt it."

Chapter Twenty-Three

"Where's Katherine?" Moriah laid the zip-locked diary on the counter and washed her hands in the sink.

Nicolas sat at the kitchen table, his laptop in front of him. "Upstairs in our room. She has a headache."

"Is she okay?"

"She's fine."

Moriah noticed that he was frowning as he stared at the laptop.

"We finished the cottage today." Moriah was proud of what they'd accomplished. "The floor is completely finished and it is gorgeous. Jack and the others did such a good job on it. The only thing left now is installing the big windows in the lantern room and rigging some sort of light. Oh, and if you don't mind, I'd like to purchase an excellent telescope. The lantern room needs one. When the weather is good, you'll be able to see for miles up there."

Nicolas ignored her.

"What are you looking at?" She searched for a towel, but the one Katherine usually kept near the sink was missing. "You seem concerned."

"I am. Ben sent me an e-mail."

Her heart nearly stopped. "Is something wrong?"

"He doesn't sound coherent."

She dried her hands on her jeans and bent over Nicolas' shoulder to take a look.

"It's as though he's hallucinating or something. The message is gar-bled and misspelled," Nicolas said.

"Ben doesn't misspell words."

"I know. That's why I'm worried. Here, read it for yourself."

The message was short and disturbing.

kum fast ben bad hot

"What in the world?" Moriah said.

"I don't know. I sent a reply and I'm waiting for an answer." Nicolas forked his fingers through his hair. "When did you last hear from him? Yesterday?"

"Actually, no. There was no message from him yesterday or last night. He had mentioned he might be visiting another tribe in a neigh-boring village. I thought perhaps he needed to stay over." Fear wrapped icy tentacles around her stomach. "What do you think is going on?"

"I don't know. But something's wrong."

He typed a sentence. "Ben. Do you have a fever?"

no ben fusiwe

"Fusiwe?" Moriah said. "Who is Fusiwe?"

"A good friend of Ben's who lives in the village. He speaks decent English, but I didn't know he could read or write yet. Apparently Ben has started teaching him."

"Is Ben sick?" Nicolas typed.

yas

Are you sick?" Nicolas asked.

no

"Ben is hot?"

bern lik fir

"Burn like fire." Moriah gripped Nicolas' shoulder. "What's happen-ing to Ben?"

"Wrap Ben in a wet sheet," Nicolas typed. "Fan him. Do not stop."

i do

"Is there a rash?"

yas

"On his face?"

no pleze kum

"High fever. A rash that hasn't spread to his face." Nicolas shook his head in dismay.

"Is it Breakbone?" he typed.

mabe

"Maybe," Moriah said. "What's Breakbone?"

"Another word for Dengue Fever."

"What's Dengue Fever?"

"The Brazilians call it 'Breakbone Fever' because a person who has it aches so badly he feels like his bones are breaking."

"How could Ben have gotten it?"

"It's mosquito borne."

"Like malaria?"

"Different mosquito. A day-biting one."

"But Ben said he was taking malaria medicine," she argued. "Wouldn't that help?"

"Not with Dengue. There's no vaccine to prevent it or medicine to cure it. The only line of defense is Deet and mosquito netting. Problem is, a man can't live his life beneath mosquito netting and it's easy enough to sweat Deet off and forget to reapply it."

"But he'll be okay?" she pleaded.

"He might." Nicolas' voice became cold and clinical, as though he were detaching himself. "As long as it doesn't turn into Hemorrhagic Fever."

"What's that?"

Nicolas didn't answer. "Fusiwe," he typed. "Is Ben bleeding?"

sum

"Where?

skn

"Under his skin?"

yas

"He's bleeding beneath his skin?" Moriah ranted. "Ben is bleeding beneath his skin! Nicolas, how bad is that?"

"It's not good."

"Do not give him aspirin," Nicolas wrote. "Keep him cool. Give him as much water as he will drink. I'm coming."

"Me too," Moriah said. "I'm coming too."

"Impossible," Nicolas said. "You don't have a passport."

"You're wrong."

"When did you get a passport?"

"While you were gone."

"You aren't ready yet."

"It doesn't matter. I'm coming."

"Think about it, Moriah. What other phobias might this trip stir up within you?"

"I'm going."

"Ben's life is at stake," Nicolas argued. "Having to stop to deal with your emotional problems isn't worth the risk. Besides, you have no medical training and I can travel more easily and quickly alone."

"I love him."

"If he is as sick as I think he is, he won't even know you're there."

"I can *fix* things!" she said. "If something breaks I can fix it."

Nicolas gave her an appraising glance. "Okay then. Sometimes there is a great need in the jungle for someone who can fix things. Go pack." He reached into the top drawer of the desk and pulled out a prescription bottle. "I got these for you last week... just in case. They are sedatives.

Pack quickly and then take one. I don't intend to deal with hysterics while we're in the air."

It was a reasonable request, although it galled her to accept Nicolas' directive. "You want to knock me out until we get there?"

"You spent exactly five whole minutes in the air before begging Bob Jr. to land the plane. Just take the pill and don't argue."

He closed the computer. "I have phone calls to make. If they go well, we can leave within the hour."

"I'll go tell Katherine," Moriah said. "She'll want to come too."

"No."

"But Katherine has medical training."

Nicolas picked up the telephone and dialed a number.

"No."

"Why?"

"Kathy's pregnant." He turned his attention to his phone conversation.

It took Moriah a moment to absorb the shock of his abrupt announcement. She heard the words "private jet" before she backed away from him and stumbled up the stairs.

The bedroom was dark, and Katherine lay on the bed with a washcloth over her eyes. Moriah stood at the doorway, calming herself before she sat down on the bed beside her aunt.

"Why didn't you tell me?" Moriah gently stroked her aunt's hair.

"Why didn't I tell you what?" Katherine pulled the washcloth away from her eyes.

"That you're pregnant."

"Oh that." Katherine waved a hand as though dismissing her concern.

"Yes, that."

"I knew you'd make a fuss."

"Well, of *course* I'll make a fuss." Moriah gazed into her aunt's eyes. "I'm worried about you. I'm so sorry this has happened to you."

"Excuse me?"

"You know, accidentally getting pregnant. At your age. I know having babies after forty is dangerous."

"You think this was an accident?" Katherine sat up and scooted against the headboard. "You are so wrong. Nicolas and I *desperately* want this child."

"You got pregnant deliberately?"

"Yes. I'm healthy as a horse, and I'm perfectly capable of carrying a child full-term. The only reason I'm lying down *now* is because I have a slight headache and I don't want to take any medicine for it because of the baby."

"So, you're happy about this?"

"You'd better believe I'm happy." Katherine laid her hand over Moriah's. "Just think. I'm going to have a *baby*! I'm so happy I can't even talk about it without crying."

"Is Nicolas pleased?"

"Ecstatic."

"Nicolas? Ecstatic?"

"Yes, Moriah. Ecstatic. He just doesn't jump up and down to show it."

"When are you due?"

"June."

"You guys didn't waste much time."

"We knew we wanted a child." Katherine shrugged. "As you keep pointing out, I *am* past forty."

"Okay, if you're happy, I'm happy. But I can't talk anymore about this right now. Ben is sick and Nicolas and I are leaving for the Amazon within the hour."

Katherine grasped her by the arm. "What's wrong?"

"Nicolas thinks Ben may have Dengue Fever."

"That can be fatal!"

"I know. Will you help me pack?"

"Of course!" Katherine was suddenly all business; headache and pregnancy temporarily forgotten. "You already have some jungle gear selected, don't you?"

"I've been getting things ready. They're in my closet."

They hurried to her room and began filling a nylon backpack with cotton underclothes, quick-drying shorts, pants, socks, hiking boots and t-shirts. Katherine went to her own room and came back with a handful of energy bars that she shoved into a side pocket.

"Where did you get those?" Moriah asked.

"I seem to be hungry all the time since I became pregnant. You'll need these. I can get more."

"Moriah!" Nicolas called from the bottom of the stairs. "You ready?"

"Doesn't he need to pack too?" Moriah asked.

"Nicolas keeps a packed bag in his car and another one in his plane at all times," Katherine said. "He's like a boy scout, always prepared."

Katherine's "boy scout" appeared in the door, his expression grim and determined. "The weather is good. I'll fly my plane to the Toronto island airport. There will be an Extended Range Leer jet fueled and readied by the time we get there."

Moriah slid the passport she had recently obtained into a side pocket of her bag and zipped everything up.

"Don't forget this." Nicolas tossed the bottle of medication to Moriah.

Moriah stuck it in her pocket.

"Take one now, Moriah," Nicolas said. "This trip is too important to risk you falling apart in the air. I won't order the pilot to land if you have a meltdown."

Moriah opened the vial, tossed one capsule in her mouth and swallowed. The capsule stuck in her throat. She pushed past Nicolas to go into the bathroom, filled a glass, threw her head back and drank until the pill reached her stomach.

She sat the glass down, gripped the sides of the sink, looked at the mirror and stared into her own eyes. Even if she had to stay sedated the whole way, no matter what it took, she *would* go to Ben.

Moriah ran down to where Nicolas' pontoon sat in the water, fully aware that she would be traveling across Lake Huron, the continental United States, a portion of the ocean and deep into a South American jungle.

Nicolas stowed her bag as she buckled herself into the seat, grasped the armrests with an iron grip, and whispered. "Stay alive, my love."

Then she squeezed her eyes closed, clamped her jaw, and fought her desire to scream as the seaplane lifted into the air.

Chapter Twenty-Four

The capsule she had swallowed back at the lodge had begun to work its magic by the time Nicolas landed at the Toronto island airport. At least Moriah thought that was what was happening. She definitely didn't feel like herself. She also thought it was a sad state of affairs when not feeling like yourself was a *good* thing.

The private jet they boarded looked powerful enough to carry them non-stop to Honduras, where Nicolas said they'd refuel before flying to the airport nearest to the Yahnowa. The smell of expensive leather laced with jet fuel permeated the cabin.

"The weather looks clear most of the way," the pilot said. "With a bit of tail wind, we could make it into Sao Paulo in nine or ten hours."

"Radio ahead, please, and see if you can make arrangements for a helicopter to take us the rest of the way," Nicolas instructed. "A pilot by the name of Ron Meacham picked up a missionary and his wife awhile ago. The temporary clearing the tribe created might still be open."

"I'll check, but the jungle closes up fast," the pilot warned.

"I know," Nicolas said.

Moriah ran a hand over the glove-soft leather of her seat after she'd buckled herself in. "What does renting a jet like this cost?"

"A lot." Nicolas said.

"What's 'a lot?'"

"I've delivered hundreds of babies, Moriah. Some of those

pregnancies were extremely high risk. Fathers can be quite grateful when you save the life of their wife and child. Tonight I called in a favor."

"Thank you for doing this, Nicolas."

"You're welcome, but I'm not doing this for you."

The plane was so luxurious that she felt slightly apologetic for even sitting in the lovely leather seats. With Katherine's help, she had stuffed a bag full of clothes and necessities, but she had not taken the time to change out of the clothes she had worked in all day. Every minute was too valuable.

"Is the medication still working?" Nicolas asked, as she felt the jet start down the runway."

"I think so. I'm more sleepy than scared."

"Good." Nicolas pulled a blanket out of a storage cabinet. "Then sleep as long as you can." He handed her the blanket. "If Ron isn't available, or if his old helicopter is out of commission again, or if the landing area they cleared for Violet has closed up, we might have to hike in. It's best to be well-rested before you do that."

"What about you? Don't you need to rest?" She spread the blanket over her legs and leaned her seat back. She heard the jet engine start up. The medication had definitely taken the edge off. That and the fact that the jet was so elegant and well-appointed that it felt like being seated in a small living room. She thought that, if she pretended really hard, she could almost convince herself that it wasn't a plane at all.

"I don't require much sleep," he said. "I learned to go without when I was delivering babies."

The jet began to roll down the runway. As she gripped the armrests and closed her eyes, another repressed memory bubbled up.

The priest was kind, but he was a stranger. She wished Mommy or Daddy were there to hold her as the big airplane roared off into the sky. She did not want the priest to hold her and he did not offer. She felt small and very alone as she sat in the seat beside him and stared out the window. After a while she needed to go to the bathroom, but she was afraid to go there by herself. Being on the plane with this man who dressed funny was so alien to her that she couldn't make herself ask him to take her. So she simply waited. And waited. Until it was too late.

The priest was surprised when they stood up to leave the plane and discovered that her clothing and seat were wet. He waited until everyone else had left the airplane, then he called the stewardess over and quietly told her what had happened. The stewardess was unhappy about the wet seat and frowned at her. The priest held Moriah's hand as he led her off the plane.

It felt awful walking out of the plane with wet clothes. She glanced back over her shoulder and saw there were now two stewardesses shaking their heads over the wet seat. She knew from the expressions on their faces that she had done something very bad.

Moriah felt her stomach lurch as the jet lifted from the ground, but that was all she remembered. A prescription drug-induced sleep took over, deep and dreamless.

Chapter Twenty-Five

Moriah awoke with a start, disoriented. She was surprised to discover it was dark. It had been daylight when she fell asleep. Where was she?

The only light was a dim one directly above Nicolas' head. He looked neat and professional as he worked at a small desk. Vaguely she remembered getting on the jet with him.

A jet! She was in the air?

She scrambled to sit up and glanced out the window beside her seat. The inky space outside the jet's window was relieved only by stars. She didn't like this feeling of flying at night. In Bob Jr.'s piper cub, she had at least been able to look out the window and anchor herself with familiar landmarks.

Being inside a Leer Jet, at night, was nothing like flying with Bob Jr. Nor was it anything like the large commercial jet she'd ridden in as a child—which had felt cavernous to her. This tightly built, encapsulated craft was beginning to make her feel as though she was inside a tomb. As full realization came of where they were, she broke out in a cold sweat, and her stomach heaved. She pressed her forehead against the cool glass of the window and tried to force the nausea down.

Nicolas glanced over at her with concern. "Get up, Moriah. You're turning green."

She couldn't make herself move. He jumped up and half-carried her to the miniscule bathroom.

She lost the contents of her stomach into the toilet while Nicolas held her long hair out of her face.

When there was nothing left to bring up, she flopped back against the doorframe, her stomach still spasming. Her whole body trembled from the violence of the past few minutes.

"I was afraid something like this would happen." Nicolas squatted down beside her. "Here. Rinse your mouth out." He shoved a cup of water into her hand.

She rinsed and spit into the toilet without getting up.

Nicolas was annoyed. "I have half a mind to leave you off in Honduras when we land for gas."

"No!" She still felt sick, but her will to go to Ben remained unchanged. "I'm going with you. I don't care how many times I get sick. I'll just keep going."

"Where's your medication? Obviously, it's worn off. Take another pill."

She searched her pockets. "I don't have it."

"You've got to be kidding."

"I—I think I left it on the bathroom sink back home."

Nicolas' face was a study of resignation. "Of course you did. Nothing is ever easy with you."

"I'm okay. I can do this." Moriah stretched out on the carpeted floor, her head a few inches from the bathroom door. Lying there, she felt slightly less nauseous than sitting in a seat, staring out at the dark sky. With her head against the carpeted floor, she could also hear the comforting thrum of a well-kept engine.

"I'm okay," she repeated, closing her eyes.

She heard a snap, then a fizz and, when she opened her eyes again, she saw Nicolas bringing her a can of ginger ale. He grabbed a pillow from an overhead compartment and handed both items to her.

Gratefully, she sat up and sipped the soda. "Thanks."

"You're welcome."

When she'd finished her drink, Moriah lay back down on the floor with her pillow and felt marginally better. She tried to distract herself by concentrating on plans for her wedding. It was easier to visualize getting married in the beautiful lighthouse cottage, than to think about Ben fighting for his life right now with no one but a young tribesman caring for him. Emotionally exhausted, she finally dozed once again, waking only briefly when Nicolas tucked a blanket around her.

Chapter Twenty-Six

....

Hours later, Moriah watched as Nicolas perused a faded map along with Ron Meacham and Ron's co-pilot son, Matt. The map was tacked onto the wall of a rickety plywood airport hanger. Ron's gray hair was cut military short and he wore a spotless white shirt with pressed khaki pants. His face was tanned and creased with years of squinting into the sun. Matt was simply a younger carbon copy of his dad.

The tropical sun blazed down on the corrugated tin roof, which made the hanger feel like a sauna. She felt slow and dumb, as though her mind was starting to shut down from having too much to process.

In less than a day, she had come from a Canadian late summer with the crisp snap of autumn in the air, to this oppressive South American heat. She couldn't remember ever being so unbearably warm. The weight of the moisture-laden air was suffocating. She tried to tune back into the conversation, but it was difficult to concentrate.

"You're sure?" Nicolas folded up the map.

"The jungle grows back so fast," Ron said. "Unless the tribe has kept it clear, it will be next to impossible to land."

"How close can you take us in then?" Nicolas asked.

Moriah swayed slightly. The combination of weariness and heat was making her dizzy.

Nicolas glanced at her. "We'd better get her out of this hothouse. Ron, let's get there and circle the village. If the landing place isn't clear, I know there's a tribe a few miles directly to the south that Ben has visited. There's a large landing field not too far from there that a lumber company uses. It wouldn't be too hard to walk the rest of the way."

"Normally that would be a good idea," Matt said. "But not right now. There's been some unrest again there the past couple weeks. The lumber company left until things settled down. That tribe is not up to welcoming company right now."

"Our 'copter carries enough fuel to circle Mrs. Smith's clearing and get back here," Ron said. "If it's clear, we'll land. If it isn't we'll come back and figure something else out."

"Sounds like a plan." Nicolas shouldered his bag of medical supplies. "I'm ready."

Moriah felt better outside the hanger. She followed the three men to where an army-green helicopter was tethered. Unfortunately, the aircraft looked quite a bit worse for wear. In fact, in her opinion, it looked like it should be sold for scrap.

"How old is this craft?" she asked.

"Our Huey?" Ron said. "It flew in Vietnam. We picked it up from war surplus."

"Then that would explain the bullet holes?"

"It was a mess when we got it. Matt and I had our work cut out for us, but it purrs like a kitten now."

"A kitten that has to cough up a hairball every now and then." Matt laughed. "There's still a few small mechanical kinks we need to work out—nothing for you to worry about—but we're making progress."

Moriah stared at it with dismay. With Nicolas' seaplane and with the Leer jet she had confidence in the crafts, even if she didn't have any confidence in herself. However, with this Huey, she had grave misgivings. She wished she could take a long, hard look at that Huey engine, but there wasn't time.

Matt slid the side door open, pulled out a vest, helmet, headset and goggles then handed them to her.

"I'm supposed to wear all this?" she asked.

"Standard procedure." He helped her slip the vest over her arms. "We'll be following the Amazon river for part of the trip. If we go down in the water, pull this nozzle on the container of pressurized oxygen you have here on this pocket, and the vest will inflate."

"And that will save me?"

"Sure, unless a croc or piranhas get to you. Try to swim fast and get onto land as quickly as possible."

"Okay." Moriah tried to keep her voice from shaking.

He placed the helmet on her head and helped her adjust the goggles. "This will keep the bugs out of your eyes."

"Bugs?"

"We keep the doors open for ventilation when we fly."

Moriah repeated his words like a parrot. "Doors open. Ventilation. Life vest. Oxygen. Crocodiles. Piranhas."

The panic was rising and she wasn't even off the ground yet.

Nicolas read the desperation on her face.

"You'll be fine," he said. "Ron is famous in this area for getting into and out of tough places. He knows what he's doing."

Matt climbed into the Huey and folded a canvas and aluminum seat down from the wall.

"Get in and sit down," he said.

Moriah got in and sat down.

Together, he and Nicolas strapped Moriah into her seat.

"This is an intercom." Matt said, as he plugged a long wire from her helmet into the electrical system of the helicopter. "Push the button here on the wire if you want to talk to any of us while we're in flight."

"Push button," she repeated, her head spinning.

In the other two aircraft, it had been possible to close her eyes and at least *try* to pretend that she was inside a safe little room. In this too-open helicopter there was no possibility of pretending. There was no carpeting, no soft music, no luxurious leather seats. There weren't even any *doors*, for crying out loud.

Nicolas, clad in the same type of life vest and helmet as the others, calmly buckled himself in while Matt climbed into the co-pilot's seat.

She saw them flipping switches, and then the high-pitched whine of the engines slowly started up and the blades began to turn. She could smell the fumes. She didn't know if that was the exhaust of burnt fuel or hydraulic fluid. Neither pilot reacted or seemed concerned, so she assumed it was normal.

Soon the popping sound of the blades on the Huey began and then escalated. The sound became deafening where she was sitting. She felt every pop like an impact against her chest as the old bird began to vibrate. Her body tensed as the blades became a blur and then the ancient beast lifted into the air.

The aircraft bounced once as it rose and hovered above the trees, then Ron slanted the blades to bite into the air and they moved forward at an alarming angle, pitching Moriah sharply against her seat straps. The single pill she had taken to placate Nicolas had definitely worn off. Now, she was protected by nothing, not even by the blanket of night. She could see quite well, unfortunately.

As Ron headed toward the Yahnowa village, wind rushed at her through the open door as the valiant motor of the old military craft roared in her ears. Although the helicopter wasn't moving anywhere close to the same speed that the jet had flown, it somehow felt like it was flying faster as she absorbed every vibration, every bounce and every shimmy.

The sensory overload, after staying on the island for over twenty years, was overwhelming. She had had enough. Everything was moving too fast, rushing toward her, like the wind that kept whipping against her from the open doors. The fear was unbearable, filling her mind with so much pain that she didn't know if she could bear it. She could hear Matt, Ron and Nicolas talking to one another through the speaker inside her helmet, but she didn't comprehend what they were saying. She was too absorbed in fighting her own, intense battle.

The helicopter felt like a fragile eggshell as it chopped its way over a coffee-colored river snaking its way through an ocean of green vegetation. Sometimes Ron flew the helicopter so low, she feared that the treetops would scrape its belly.

Her fear escalated into sheer terror.

She fought against the desire to rip off the helmet and tear off the seat harness. Although there was no lack of fresh air, she found herself having difficulty catching her breath. In an attempt to regain emotional control, she bit the inside of her cheek until it bled, clenched her fists until her fingernails made cuts into her palm, grabbed her hair with both hands and pulled as hard as she could—focusing on the pain she was inflicting on herself—trying to concentrate on anything except the most dizzying, heart-palpitating, paralyzing terror she had ever experienced.

After what felt like two eternities, she saw Nicolas tense and lean forward.

"There's the village!" Nicolas shouted, pointing.

They were here? They'd made it? Moriah glanced down. There was a tiny village of huts below them. The village looked like a small sore that had opened up inside the rolling green carpet of healthy vegetation that stretched as far as her eyes could see. People, who from her vantage point looked like dark ants, were pointing up and running toward a spot directly beneath where the helicopter was now hovering.

"Son of a… biscuit eater!"

She had a strong feeling that Ron had intended to say something besides 'biscuit eater' but changed his mind at the last minute.

Nicolas hung his head outside the door and looked down.

"What?" She leaned forward. "What's wrong?"

"Bamboo can grow more than a foot a day in the jungle. I gambled that the villagers would keep the clearing open. They did not."

"Looks like they are making an attempt now," Matt said.

It was true. In an area that looked slightly less dense than the rainforest canopy all around them, several villagers were hacking away at the new growth. It looked like difficult work because the bamboo towered far above their heads. Their efforts were too little, too late.

"Fusiwe must have told them we were coming," Nicolas' voice was frustrated. "But they haven't had time to make enough progress. We can't land in this."

"But they are trying to clear it." Being so close to Ben and unable to land was maddening. "Can't we give them a little more time?"

"How much fuel do we have left?" Nicolas asked Ron.

"Just over half a tank. It was full when we left. If we don't have any problems we can make it back to Sao Paulo, but just barely. This old bird is thirstier than usual today. We'll need to do something to fix that when we get back."

"We can't turn back," Moriah said. "Ben is in that village. Don't helicopters have ropes or something they use to rescue people?"

"Sorry, sweetheart," Ron said. "We aren't equipped for that. Nick—do you think Ben can survive waiting a day or two for the villagers to finish working on the clearing?"

"Probably not." Nicolas glanced at her.

"Well then," Ron said. "If that's the case, it's time for an old trick I learned from a buddy back in Nam. Best pilot I ever knew. Scared the bejeebers out of me the only time I ever saw it."

"Dad?" Matt sounded worried. "What are you doing?"

"I'm turning this old bird into a weed-whacker!" Ron roared. "It might be a one-way trip, but if it's Ben's only chance I gotta try. I like that boy. Always have."

Ron hovered over the landing area for a few seconds to make it clear to the people below that he was coming in while Matt and Nicolas gestured frantically for the villagers to get out of the way.

Moriah felt the Huey being lowered further and further until suddenly the blades began biting into the bamboo and debris flew everywhere.

Bits and pieces of vegetation started pelting her and she instinctively covered her eyes with her hands. The sound of flying bamboo striking the metal of the helicopter was thunderous.

Finally, with a hard thump, the Huey touched earth and Ron slowed the rotation of the blades.

Someone pried Moriah's hands away from her face. She opened her eyes and saw Nicolas staring at her with concern. She glanced around, dazed and uncertain.

"I'm okay," she said. "I think. Are you?"

"I'm fine." Nicolas brushed pieces of leaves off his shirt. "We're here now. Let's go."

Nicolas climbed out of the helicopter while the blades continued to turn. She hurriedly pulled her helmet, goggles and headset off, unbuckled her seat belt and slid out of the helicopter. While they waited for Matt to join them, she silently blessed the fact that she was once again standing on firm ground.

"So," Nicolas said, dryly. "Did you enjoy your first helicopter ride?"

Chapter Twenty-Seven

Moriah felt as drained as if she had run a marathon... twice. The earth around her was littered with pieces of leaves and bamboo.

"Matt, would you grab the stretcher?" Nicolas asked.

"Got it," Matt said.

"I'm staying with the Huey," Ron said. "I'm afraid we might have sustained a bit of damage. If I turn it off it might not start up again."

"Will it take us out of here?" Nicolas asked.

"Hope so," Ron said. "But it wasn't made for what I just did to it."

Villagers began to cautiously emerge from the forest where they had hidden to escape the rainfall of bamboo.

"Might be a good idea to hurry," Ron shouted, his voice strained as he stared up at the rotating blades.

Instead of just the solid sound of rotors beating the air, Moriah heard an eerie sort of whistling. It sounded like it was coming from the Huey's blades but she couldn't be sure.

In what sounded like halting Yahnowa, Nicolas quickly greeted and thanked the villagers, then shouldered his medical bag and strode forward.

"Follow directly behind me, Moriah," he instructed. "Don't touch anything. If you fall, make sure you fall straight down onto the path. Whatever you do, don't try to grab onto anything to break your fall."

"Why?" Moriah was still coveting the feel of firm ground beneath her feet and fighting the urge to hug the nearest tree.

"Because it might be alive and deadly, sharp as a razor, or filled with poison. Ignorance can get you killed very quickly in the jungle."

"Oh." Suddenly, the lush beauty of the place felt threatening. "I'll be careful."

"Don't let him scare you." Matt brought up the rear as they walked beneath the rainforest canopy. "You'll learn what to touch and what to avoid. It's not really that hard. It's just that you don't know anything yet. Nicolas is right. Ignorance can be deadly in the jungle."

She stuck her hands firmly in her pockets to remind herself not to use them if she tripped and fell. It would be tough.

After a short hike, they arrived at the small village. Nicolas headed straight toward a hut that looked like it had been made from dried grass. It sat slightly outside the others. As they entered, she saw Ben. He lay as still as death, his body on a raised platform of bamboo, his body swathed in a wet sheet.

On the flight to Sao Paulo, she had prayed for a miraculous recovery. She had hoped that Ben would somehow be able to welcome her with open arms, laughing about her great fear for him. One glance, and she knew that would not be happening. Not this time. Ben was completely unconscious. His face was flushed, his breathing ragged. A rash covered the upper part of his chest. He did not show any sign of knowing that she and Nicolas were there.

An exhausted-looking young tribesman stood over Ben, fanning him with a palm leaf.

"Fusiwe." Nicolas' voice was respectful. "How is our friend?"

"Not good. I kept wet sheets on him all night," the young tribesman said. "Rashawe helped. He spent much time putting drops of water into Ben's mouth."

Moriah was surprised that the young man spoke English so well.

From the misspelled email, she had expected Fusiwe's English to be practically incoherent. Evidently, he had only recently begun his spelling lessons.

"Are others in the village affected?"

"Three. They all went with Ben to another village. Bad mosquitos there. Two died. Many villagers stay in their huts now; afraid."

"Talk to them," Nicolas said. "Explain that Dengue isn't contagious. Is Ben better or worse than he was yesterday?"

"Worse."

Nicolas quickly examined Ben, then turned to her. "We have to get him to the hospital as fast as possible. I'll start an IV as soon as we get back to the helicopter. Let's move!"

Chapter Twenty-Eight

....

Matt and Fusiwe held the canvas stretcher steady while Nicolas and Moriah muscled Ben off his pallet and onto it. Ben was so solid, it took all her strength to help lift him. Once they got him secured, Matt and Fusiwe took off on a fast walk through the jungle with Ben's limp, fever-ridden body between them.

Moriah's mind was leaping ahead, making calculations as she and Nicolas followed. At best, it would take maybe five minutes to load him, strap him in and get into the air. Nicolas would start the IV that had been among the medical supplies a doctor friend had placed on the private jet before they left. Thanks to Nicolas, they had gotten here in time. Soon they would be at the hospital where Ben would have a fighting chance.

Fusiwe helped load Ben into the helicopter, got out from under the still rotating blades and then stood in the shade of the forest while Matt and Nicolas secured the stretcher and Ben as well. Then she crawled into the helicopter and knelt beside him.

Ben's face was so unnaturally pale. She smoothed back his unruly red hair and kissed his forehead. Her lips registered the heat. He was burning up. How long could his body sustain a fever like this? His eyelids did not so much as flicker at her touch.

Nor did he flinch when the IV needle went in. Nicolas hung the bag of life-saving liquid on a hook that appeared to have been attached to the

Huey for that very purpose. Moriah held Ben's hand and wondered how many other lives this old helicopter had saved.

"We're getting you help, my love," she said. "You're going to be okay."

Nicolas buckled himself in and donned his helmet, goggles and headset.

Once again Ron and Matt started flipping switches and the whine of the engine escalated. As the blades began to rotate faster, that troubling whistling sound she had noted earlier increased.

Ron looked back at them. His face was deadly serious. He said something into his mic and Nicolas' head snapped back as though he had just received a blow. He glanced worriedly at her, still kneeling beside Ben.

While the men communicated with one another she made her way to her seat, donned her helmet and plugged in her headset. Something was wrong and she wanted to know what it was.

She interrupted their conversation. "What's going on?"

"Ron and I have decided that you need to get off the helicopter, Moriah," Nicolas said.

"Why?"

"For your own safety."

Ron's voice interrupted Nicolas. "The hydraulic pressure is low. It will be running hot soon. The fuel needle is barely past a half of a tank. You need to get off."

"But…"

She tried to argue, but Ron wasn't interested. He jerked a thumb at the open door.

"Out!"

"I don't understand. I'm want to be with Ben."

"We don't need your weight adding stress to the 'copter," Ron said. "Out!"

She glanced around at the inside the helicopter and keyed her mic.

"That's ridiculous. This thing was built to hold at least a dozen soldiers. My weight isn't going to make any difference."

"Please leave, Moriah," Nicolas said. "Fusiwe will take you back to the village."

"No," she said. "I'm staying with Ben."

The whistling sound continued.

Ron threw his headset down, climbed out of the helicopter and came around to the open door beside her. He was a man of few words. Without asking, he unbuckled her restraints and tried to pull her out of the open door as the blades picked up speed.

Even as she clawed at the seat to keep from being dragged off, it struck her that only yesterday she would have fought anyone who tried to make her get on one of these things. Now, she was fighting to stay on.

All because of Ben.

Love did, indeed, overcome fear.

Vaguely, through the headset, she heard Matt's voice talking fast. "The bird is damaged, Moriah. The blades are compromised. Some of the steel is missing. The honeycomb structure beneath has been exposed, which is why the blades are whistling. The hydraulics *are* low and will be running hot soon. That means we'll burn even more fuel going back than coming. There is a chance we might not make it. There's no reason for you to be at risk too."

"But…"

"If anything happens to us," Nicolas said. "I need you to go home and take care of Kathy and the baby. I'm begging you. Get off the helicopter. Now!"

Her heart plummeted. Nicolas was right. Katherine would need her. She had to get off.

With tears streaming down her face, she let go of the doorframe. Ron staggered backward two steps at her quick release. Then, realizing she had given up, he went back to the cockpit and climbed in. She tore off her headset, goggles and helmet as Nicolas threw her bag out after her.

The wounded metal bird immediately flew into the air.

Once again, Ben was leaving her behind.

Chapter Twenty-Nine

Moriah watched in silence as the helicopter turned into a speck in the sky and the sound of rotors evaporated.

She heard someone cough, and realized it was Fusiwe trying to get her attention. She turned and looked at him—this man who had saved Ben's life. Fusiwe wore nothing but a breechcloth. His hair was long and plaited down his back. Moriah glanced down at her blue jeans, sweat-soaked t-shirt and tennis shoes. In spite of her intense worry about Ben, if she was going to be under Fusiwe's care, she thought it best to start things off on an honest footing.

"I'm dumb as dirt. I don't even know how to feed myself here."

"I know," Fusiwe said. "Follow me. And do not *touch* anything!"

She wiped the tears from her cheeks with the tail of her t-shirt, picked up her bag, then obediently followed him, arms stiffly down at her side. Things had taken a turn she could never have anticipated. How would she know if they had made it safely to the hospital? What would she do if they didn't?

In the meantime, her life pretty much depended on the man walking the path in front of her.

"Thank you for taking care of him," she said. "If it weren't for you, we wouldn't even know he was sick."

"Ben is my friend," Fusiwe said.

"How did you learn to speak English?"

"Violet and Abraham teach me. Ben teach me Portuguese, too. It is the language of Brazil and valuable to know."

"So you speak three languages?"

"Four. Ben teach me Spanish, too."

"Four languages?" Moriah said. "Why?"

Fusiwe stopped in the middle of the path, turned around and looked at her as though she might be a little stupid. "To protect my people, of course."

"How will learning all these languages help protect the Yahnowa?"

"Ben says knowing the language of the people around us gives us power. Especially if they think we are ignorant. My wife and my wife's brother, Rashawe, learn too. We are not ignorant."

"I thought you were still pretty isolated here."

"Yes, for now. I fear we cannot be isolated much longer. The farmers eat away at our land. They clear it with fire and grow crops, but the soil is thin. It only supports a few plantings. Then it gets tired and the crops do not thrive. The farmers move on. Ben prepares us to survive in the future as well as give us a Bible translation."

"Nicolas says you're some sort of apprentice to the local witch doctor?"

The young man winced, then he turned and continued down the path. "The correct word is Shaman. Yes, I'm learning to be a healer. In our ignorance and need, my people turned to what you might call witchcraft. I am not interested in chants and magical spells, but I *am* interested in what there is to be learned from the old people who have much knowledge about herbs and plants."

"Did I offend you?" Moriah reached out to touch an exotic-looking flower, but remembered at the last moment to jerk her hand back. "I didn't mean to."

"I am not offended, but I am tired. I care for Ben for two days. Before that my people need my help."

He stopped outside a neatly built hut and called softly. A lovely young woman peeked out at Moriah with brown eyes as soft and lovely as a young doe.

"This is my wife." Fusiwe wearily entered his one-room hut. "She take care of you." He climbed into a hammock, closed his eyes and fell asleep immediately.

It was obvious that caring for Ben had taken quite a toll on the man.

"Hello." Moriah wondered how much his wife understood. She had long, shiny black hair much the same as Moriah's, but she wore little in the way of clothing except swirls of paint.

"You have green eyes!" The woman stepped closer, touching Moriah's face. It felt strange having another woman caress her face, but Moriah thought perhaps it was one of those strange tribal customs she might have to get used to.

"A friend of my childhood had eyes this green. Ben says you are my childhood friend."

Moriah's eyes opened wide. "Karyona?"

The young woman nodded and smiled.

Moved beyond words, Moriah embraced her, paint and all.

"We always wondered about you," Karyona said. "We worry about you many years."

Fusiwe stirred restlessly in his sleep. Karyona looked at him with concern.

"Our voices disturb him. Should we go to Ben's hut to talk?"

"Good idea," Moriah said.

After they arrived at Ben's place, they climbed onto his sleeping platform and continued their conversation.

"I would have gotten word to you if I had known." Moriah stared at her friend in wonder. "But I had no memory of anything that happened here until a few months ago. Is your father and mother still living?"

"Oh yes. He is on a long hunting trip. My mother visits relatives in a different tribe. They will come back in a few days. Until then, we have much to talk about."

Chapter Thirty

The two women stayed late in Ben's hut, facing each other, sitting cross-legged on his sleeping platform, whispering as the years fell away. Moriah felt the same gentleness emanating from Karyona that she had felt as a child.

"Why didn't Ben tell me about you?" Moriah said. "After he got the satellite computer, we were in contact nearly every day."

"He was afraid you might not want to see me again for fear it would bring back more bad memories, and he wants so much for you to come here."

"You are a happy memory, Karyona. Not a bad one."

"Do you remember Little Man?" Her friend smiled. "I think he is a happy memory."

"My monkey? Of course! I loved him. I was so proud that I had a monkey for a pet. Whatever happened to him?"

"We cared for him until he die of old age. He have a good life."

"Thank you for doing that. How's your brother?"

"Rashawe?" Karyona's face lit up. "He does well. His wife is with child. We are happy to welcome another little one into our village."

"He put his life at risk to save me. So did your father."

"They are warriors. It was what they are born to do. Moawa's attack was a surprise to them. If they knew, he and his followers would never make it to your parents'."

Moriah shivered involuntarily at even hearing the name Moawa.

Karyona touched Moriah's arm with concern. "You are still frightened of him?"

"Yes."

"I was too," Karyona said. "Until he came out of the hills begging food."

Moriah stared. "What?"

"Moawa is blind and very helpless now."

"You mean he's *here*?" Moriah jumped off the sleeping platform and whirled around as though expecting Moawa to pounce at her from some dark corner.

"He can no longer hurt anyone, Moriah. You do not need to fear him."

"Where is he?"

"Our villagers never forgave him for what he did. Because of him, we lost the good doctor as well as your family. But he was once a headman, and he is blind. A village meeting was held and it was decided to build him a hut far outside the village. We isolated him to punish him for what he had done, but we still provide water and food. He does not have a happy life, Moriah."

"I can't believe Ben never told me!"

"Perhaps, again, he was afraid you would never come to him if you knew."

"It would have made it harder for me to do so," Moriah admitted.

"Would you like to go see him?"

"Moawa? No! Absolutely not."

"I think it would be wise. He is no monster now."

"I can't, Karyona. I just can't."

"I understand." Karyona slid off the bamboo platform. "I will leave you to rest now. You have had a long day. We will see each other in the morning." She smiled as she left. "I am so glad you are here, my sister."

After Karyona's departure, Moriah ran her hand over a primitive desk Ben had made from wooden crates and boards. The satellite laptop was in the middle. It was here that Ben had sat, writing to her about his world and his life. It was attached to what looked like a car battery. She wondered who had carried the heavy object here.

The kerosene lamp she had lit cast shadows all about her. The jungle rose in a cacophony of sounds as nocturnal carnivores went about their grisly business. Next door to her there was a cough, then a child called out in its sleep. She heard the sounds of a mother soothing it.

This had been Ben's world for five years while he patiently worked at bringing the written word to these people, along with the languages that would help equip the young adults of the village to communicate with the outside world if necessary.

His Bible lay in front of her. The one he'd used back on the island. It was well worn, its spine held together with silver duct tape. She traced a finger across the cover. She had wanted to buy him a new one, but he had said he liked this one best because he knew where everything was in it.

Beside his Bible lay a fresh spiral notebook filling up with the language she knew to be Yahnowa. She riffled through the last pages. His handwriting had grown sloppy toward the end, as though he had tried to continue in spite of the fever.

Apparently, her lionhearted Ben had been trying to finish the translation so he could come back to her if, after all, she wasn't able to make herself come to him.

Beside the translation notebook was another, smaller one. She opened it, wanting any small piece of him with which to comfort herself. As she read the first page, she realized that this was his prayer diary. She had not known Ben wrote down his prayers, but it did not surprise her.

What did surprise her were the words.

"Father, she is more beautiful than any woman I've ever known. I dream about her at night and think about her all day. I've memorized the scent of her hair and the perfection of her eyelashes. I don't know what the future holds for us, if anything, but I know this much—she hurts, Lord. Please take the pain, whatever it is, from her heart."

Tears crowded her vision as she checked the date. May 10th. Two days after Ben had arrived on Manitoulin. Long before he could have had the faintest inkling about her past. But he had seen into her heart, anyway.

Brushing away the tears, she read on.

Father, would you mind blinding her to my faults and teach her to see me with loving eyes? I don't think I'm going to want to live without her.

Moriah smiled. Ben had been coercing God behind her back. No wonder she had fallen in love with him so quickly. Ben didn't play fair.

Fascinated, she read on—the details of their journey together chronicled on these pages. Sometimes she laughed, sometimes she cried, but the final pages made her sit up.

Lord God, I'm afraid Moriah will never forgive me for bringing Moawa to this village, but I didn't know what else to do. When I found him, he was wandering alone, sightless, half-starved. His own tribe decimated by disease. What could I do? Watch another human being suffer? I cannot tell her. And yet I must. If only she could see him; could see that her monster no longer exists.

Moriah frowned. No way was she going to set eyes on Moawa. He could stay in his hut out there in the jungle until he rotted, as far as she was concerned.

She was so exhausted; even the thin mat on Ben's bamboo bed looked good to her. It was probably still drenched in his sweat, but she was too tired to care. Everything felt damp anyway, including her own clothes. There was mosquito netting above, but apparently it had not been enough to save Ben from the toxic mosquito that had bit him.

Mosquito repellent sat on a shelf. She splashed it on liberally. Then she blew out the kerosene lamp, lowered the mosquito netting around her and lay in the dark. Eventually she fell into a fitful sleep, rousing at every sound. A child's cough, a puma's growl, the snapping of a twig, all wove themselves into a pattern that melded and blended and swirled with dreams in which her father, Ben, and Petras fought barehanded with a giant chieftain wielding a gleaming machete.

She awakened in the early morning hours, drenched in sweat. Her bladder was crying out to be emptied and she didn't know where to go. There were no windows; the only opening was the door, but from the soft light that was starting to show through the small cracks in the hut's wall, she could tell that it would be dawn soon. Ben's hut didn't exactly have indoor plumbing, so if she was going to go outside to relieve herself without the entire village watching, it had to be now.

She would have been grateful to have even an outhouse to go to—but that apparently wasn't part of the culture. Presumably, the people of this tribe went in the forest, which was a place she'd repeatedly been instructed not to touch.

Carefully, she eased the door open and peeked out. No one was stirring that she could see. Quickly, she scurried around to the back of the hut and squatted in the dirt. There were times when pain overrode modesty. This was one of those times.

Quickly zipping her pants, she looked around. No one was there. No one had seen. She felt much better as she went back into Ben's hut and closed the door.

The light through the cracks in the wall gave her enough light that she didn't have to light either of the lamps. There were two gallon-sized containers marked "DRINKING WATER" sitting on the ground. She lifted one, screwed off the lid, tipped it up and sipped carefully, wishing she could turn the container of water upside down and pour it over her head to cool off. Of course that was out of the question. She needed to save it. She did not know where Ben had gotten it or how to get more. The people in the village must have a water source but, until she could find out where Ben got this, she would have to be careful.

Even though she had to be careful not to waste water, had there been any soap lying around, she would have loved to wash her face, but she couldn't find a bar anywhere. Didn't Ben bathe when he was here? Or perhaps there was a place somewhere in a river or lake where the people took their baths. Maybe they used some sort of primitive soap made from roots or berries or something. Or perhaps no one used soap in the rainforest.

Her ignorance annoyed her. She should have pestered Ben with questions about everyday things—like how to use the bathroom in the jungle without getting killed, and how to get a safe drink of water when these two gallons run out.

One thing was for certain, Ben's possessions were minimal in the extreme. There wasn't a lot to work with here, and she had packed in such a fever to get to him that dragging along something as mundane as a bar of soap simply had not occurred to her.

She felt sweaty, sticky and sleep deprived. She also felt scared and abandoned and worried about whether or not the men had made it to Sao Paulo. If they did make it, she was still worried about Ben's health.

He was strong. He was young. He would fight through this, she tried to reassure herself. But what had Fusiwe said? Two had died. One had gotten better.

Those were not great statistics.

The lack of soap was the final straw.

She felt a panic attack coming on. What was she doing here? What if Ben died? What if Nicolas didn't come back? Then in the corner, on a makeshift shelf, she spied Ben's razor, a small mirror and a ceramic soap cup with a shaving brush in it.

Pulling the cup off the shelf, she tipped a few drops of water into it and used the soft-bristled brush to make a lather. The familiar scent of Ben's favorite shaving soap wafted up and calmed her.

Completely alone, she removed her clothes and, careful not to waste a drop, poured another small amount of water on a portion of the t-shirt that she had worn all day yesterday. Using some of the lather of Ben's shaving soap, she washed her face and body the best that she could with nothing more than the dampened t-shirt.

When she was finished, she folded her t-shirt over Ben's desk chair to dry—at least as much as it would dry in the rainforest. Then she unzipped a pouch in her duffle bag and pulled out one of Katherine's energy bars. Her legs dangled from Ben's waist-high sleeping platform as she chewed and watched the light grow brighter through the cracks of the hut. The morning air felt good on her body; the menthol of Ben's soap cooled her skin.

As she surveyed the interior of Ben's home, she was impressed with the ingenuity of whoever had built this small hut with nothing more than what could be gathered in the forest. Some sort of woven grass made up the walls and roof, all of which was held up by large, bamboo poles tied together.

Her guess was that these were not structures that lasted more than a few years. Insects alone would make it unlivable eventually. Still, it impressed her.

She built with electric circular saws, battery-operated drills and lots of trips to the hardware store in Mindemoya. Her cabins, although not large, had cost quite a lot as she'd purchased the materials. Apparently, these people had built this structure with not much more than their bare hands.

With dawn approaching, she pulled fresh clothes out of her bag. The familiar smell of Katherine's fabric softener rose from the bag and brought on a wave of homesickness.

"What was I thinking?" Moriah whispered as she pulled on fresh underwear, khaki shorts and a sleeveless blue shirt. "What good did coming here do? Nicolas was right. I'm useless here."

She was sitting on Ben's bed, brushing her hair, wondering fruitlessly about Ron's helicopter. Wondering if, as hot as it was, it might be a good idea to cut her long hair short, when Karyona quietly opened the door. It was a relief to see a friendly face.

"You sleep?" Karyona said.

"A little. You?"

"Fusiwe went out again in the night. One of the village children had a bad cough."

"I heard the coughing. Was he able to help?"

"Yes. Both Fusiwe and the little one is asleep now."

"You have a good man, Karyona."

"Yes." Karyona smiled, pleased. "Are you ready to go now?"

"Go where?"

"I need to go check on Moawa and take him food. Ben and Fusiwe usually take care of his needs, and sometimes Rashawe will take a turn, but he is on a long hunt today and tomorrow, so it is up to me today. The other villagers will not go near him. I am not afraid of him, but I do not enjoy going alone. It would be nice to have a companion."

"I can't do that." Moriah shuddered. "I'm sorry."

"I know how hard it is." Karyona eyes held deep understanding. "It was difficult for me, too, the first time I went." She walked over to the bed and took one of Moriah's hands in hers. "After my father and brother took you away, my mother and I were alone for days. We were frightened. We were afraid Moawa would come to kill us for having hidden you from him. I had nightmares too."

"I'm sorry," Moriah said, and she was. The world felt a little less lonely knowing that there was at least one other person on earth who truly understood her fear, but still, she wished Karyona hadn't experienced it.

"When Ben and Fusiwe found him and brought him to our hut, I refused to stay. I shouted at them and ran away to my mother and father's hut."

"What did they do?"

"They let me cry for a while. When all my tears were gone, Ben came to me and told me the story about how Jesus had washed his friends' feet—including the friend that he knew would lead murderers to him. He asked me to try to overcome my fear so I could help him and Fusiwe do what was right. And so I did."

"Oh, Karyona," Moriah said. "Then what happened?"

"I went back to my own hut with Ben and I helped Fusiwe bathe Moawa and we put healing salve on all his cuts and scrapes. There were many. It was the hardest thing I've ever done, but I was no longer afraid of Moawa when we finished. He was so starved and shrunken. It was heartbreaking to care for his poor body. I realized that he was just a man. A scary man, maybe, at one time. But just a man."

"You are a braver woman than I am, Karyona."

"I am not. I think you can do this thing too."

"I'm not going to bathe Moawa."

"No, but you will help me go see him?"

"I can't," Moriah said. "I admire you for what you are doing, but I can't."

"I understand," Karyona said, after a short hesitation. "And it is different for me. My parents lived."

Karyona's simple words and extraordinary faith shamed Moriah.

"When I come back," Karyona said. "You may help me harvest some of my manioc crop. I think you will enjoy that."

"I would love to help you with anything," Moriah said. "As long as it does not involve seeing or dealing with Moawa."

"I will be back soon."

"Karyona?" Moriah said, before her friend could leave. "Where am I supposed to um… go to the bathroom?"

Karyona's head tilted. "Bathroom?"

"Where do I go to… relieve myself?"

"Oh," Karyona's voice was matter-of-fact. "In the forest, of course. But do not touch anything."

Chapter Thirty-One

....

Nicolas was not happy. The x-ray of Ben's chest showed that there was a buildup of fluid in his lungs. So far, Ben had been rehydrated with IV fluids along with an IV solution of electrolytes to correct the electrolyte imbalances. A transfusion of platelets had been given to try to stop the bleeding problems, but now Ben's oxygen level was abnormally low and the epidemiologist here at one of Brazil's finest hospitals was not hopeful.

"I have ordered oxygen therapy," Dr. Rodriguez said, making a quick sign of the cross. "Now, it will be in God's hands."

The doctor's statement and gesture did not surprise Nicolas. Brazil had the largest number of Catholics in the world.

Studying Ben, watching his coloring, his low oxygen levels, his continued fever—he agreed with the epidemiologist. It was, indeed, completely in God's hands now.

"You need to fight harder, my friend," Nicolas whispered to an unconscious Ben. "We've done all that we can do."

* * *

Moriah would have given anything to know if the men had made it to the hospital, but she couldn't figure out how to use Ben's satellite laptop. Fusiwe must know how to work the thing, but she had not seen him up and about yet. Even if she had been adept at using it she had no idea how to contact Nicolas. The only computer she had seen Nicolas use was the one back at the lodge. It would have been comforting to communicate with Katherine, but her aunt was not interested in such technology. After all, until now, she had Nicolas with her. They spent practically every second together. Her aunt had not possessed the need to use such things to talk to the man she loved.

Therefore, Moriah sat on Ben's chair in the middle of the morning, not knowing if Ben was alive or dead. She had initially tried to leave the door partly open for light, but so many children and adults had come to peek in at her that she had closed it because she didn't know what to do with them. No doubt, they were curious about her but, unlike Fusiwe and Karyona, they knew no English, so she couldn't talk to them.

Once she closed the door, she sat there in the semi-darkness, listening to the sounds of village voices, of which she could understand nothing. She felt useless, scared and miserable as she waited for Karyona to come back.

Karyona, the friend who had asked for her help to go see the old, blind headman. The friend who had confessed that she did not like going there alone. The friend who had asked if she would go with her.

It went against Moriah's nature not to help someone when asked. In fact, she couldn't remember ever having done so, but going to see Moawa was expecting too much. Even if it *was* Karyona who asked.

Besides that, there were practicalities involved. Katherine's stash of energy bars were not going to last forever. Moriah had been serious when she told Fusiwe that she didn't even know how to feed herself here. From a survival standpoint, alienating the only real friend she had in this place was not wise.

The possibility of having to survive here alone was starting to make the struggle she'd had crossing the bridge in Little Current look like child's play. As she hid in Ben's hut, sunk in worry about him and self-pity for herself, Karyona opened the door.

"Why do you stay in here in the dark?" Karyona said. "It is much nicer on the outside."

"I don't know anyone out there except you and Fusiwe."

"Fusiwe is in a neighboring village trying to help a man who has a sore tooth. And of course you do not know anyone else yet," Karyona smiled. "That is why you must come outside and meet my people. Will you come help me with our garden?"

"Gladly!" Moriah hopped off Ben's bed and followed Karyona. As they walked through the village, they collected a band of curious children.

Karyona stopped in front of a group of tree-like bushes, as high as her head and thick with green leaves.

"This is your garden?" Moriah asked.

"Part of it. This is my manioc grove."

"I've never seen anything like this in the gardens back on Manitoulin. How long have these plants been growing?"

"A year," Karyona said. "That is about the right amount of time for a manioc plant to grow. Here, let me show you."

Moriah watched Karyona, helped by several of the children, dig away the dirt from the roots of the first manioc plant with their hands, sticks and anything else they could use.

"Now help me pull," Karyona said.

Moriah helped her friend pull at the small tree-like plant. A clump of manioc roots, the size and shape of large, sweet potatoes was pulled away from the earth. Karyona brushed the loose dirt off with her fingers. The children, used to the spectacle of harvesting manioc roots, ran off to play.

"I will teach you how to make flour from the root," Karyona said.

"This is our most important food. You will need to know how to prepare it for Ben when he comes back. That is a wife's job."

"Okay," Moriah said. "What is the man's job?"

"The men hunt for meat."

"What kind?"

"Many things like wild pigs, monkeys, deer, jaguars and snakes."

"Snakes?"

"Yes." Karyona did not seem to find anything peculiar about eating snakes. "The men also help with fishing, although we women like to fish too. And if we are attacked, it is their job to protect us," Karyona said. "Sometimes there are raids from other tribes when they want more women. Then our men have to go fight to get us back. Our men do not want to lose their wives and daughters, so they learn to be vigilant warriors."

"How often does such a thing happen?" Moriah had a mental image of being carried through the jungle flung over some neighboring tribesman's back. Living in the rainforest was even more complicated than she'd realized.

"Not nearly as often as it did when my grandmother was young. She was kidnapped twice. My grandfather had to go fight to get her back both times."

"That was nice of him," Moriah said.

"My grandmother thought so," Karyona said. "Now, I think it would be good to fix a meal together. If you are going to be Ben's wife, you will need to know how to feed him. The forest can provide everything you need as long as you know what to use and what to avoid. Our children learn these things from the time they are small. I will teach you like a little child."

Moriah wasn't sure she liked the analogy, but she had to admit that it certainly fit.

Chapter Thirty-Two

The combination of fever medications, electrolytes, IV hydration and platelet transfusions—not to mention Ben's body's ability to heal—slowly began to take effect. For the first time since Nicolas had gotten to him, Ben opened his eyes and there was recognition in them.

"Nicolas?" he said. "What are you doing here?"

"Saving your butt." Relief flooded Nicolas' body. "Or at least the doctors and staff here at the hospital have been trying to."

"I'm in the hospital?" Ben craned his neck and tried to see out over the window sill next to his bed.

"We're in Sao Paulo," Nicolas said. "You've been deathly ill. We thought we'd lost you."

"What happened?" Ben said. "All I remember is feeling a little achy and tired and falling asleep."

"That was several days ago," Nicolas raised the head of Ben's bed so he could see outside. He knew that being able to see out of a window could help a patient who was disoriented to ground themselves. "You had a bad case of Dengue hemorrhagic fever."

"And it didn't kill me? I can't say I'm surprised I got it. With all the mosquitos that have taken a bite out of me this season, I suppose it had to happen eventually."

"I suppose."

Ben glanced outside, now that his bed had been raised. "So I'm in La Paz."

"You are," Nicolas said. "Ron and Matt helped fly you out."

"How did you get here?"

"I hired a private jet."

"Because I was sick?"

"Yes." Nicolas handed Ben a bottle of water. "Here, you still need to drink as much of this as possible."

Ben was too weak. The bottle slipped from his hand. He looked at the bottle lying on his bed, and then held up his hand and examined it. "It used to work."

Nicolas found a straw, opened the bottle, and inserted the straw into it. Then he held it while Ben swallowed several times.

"Be patient," Nicolas said. "You'll get stronger. It will take some time."

Ben laid his head back against the pillow and closed his eyes. Then he opened them as another realization hit.

"How did you know I was sick?"

"Now that's an interesting story." Nicolas gave him another sip, then sat the water bottle on the bedside table. "Fusiwe has been paying a lot more attention to your computer than you probably realized. He was able to contact me and tell me you were bad sick."

"Fusiwe did that?" Ben said. "He saved my life by contacting you?"

"He did," Nicolas said. "He also kept your fever down by keeping wet sheets on you and fanning you constantly until I could get there."

"Fusiwe is an amazing young man," Ben said. "I won't be surprised if he ends up being an emissary between the Brazilian government and the Yahnowa someday. His people are going to need someone like him."

"I can see that happening. Fusiwe would do a good job."

"How was Moriah doing when you left?" Ben took another sip.

"The last I saw her, she was with Fusiwe watching our helicopter take off. She looked okay to me, but she was not happy she couldn't come with us."

Ben sprayed water. Choked. Wiped his mouth. And looked at Nicolas wild-eyed. "Are you saying that Moriah is *here*?"

"Well not *here*, exactly," Nicolas said. "Ron's helicopter was a little iffy and I didn't want to risk the possibility of Kathy losing both of us. I made Moriah stay there in the village."

"Moriah is in the village? Alone?" Ben tried to throw back the covers so he could get out of bed. "I have to go to her!"

"You can't even lift a water bottle, Ben." Nicolas restrained him as easily as if he were a kitten. "Even if you manage to get out of this bed, you'll collapse on the floor. You haven't used those muscles for a while. Plus, you have an IV in you *and* a catheter."

Ben fell back against the pillow again. Nicolas could understand his frustration, but even that small amount of effort had caused a sheen of sweat to gather on Ben's forehead.

"She'll be fine," Nicolas said. "I'm sure Fusiwe and Karyona will take good care of her."

"You don't understand," Ben said. "Moawa is with us now. Fusiwe and I found him wandering around, blind and hungry. His villagers didn't want him anymore—they had problems of their own—and he became a burden. Our village has a long memory about what he did, and they didn't want him either. So, Rashawe, Fusiwe, Karyona and I tried to do the best we could. We fixed him a hut outside of the village and we take turns bringing him food and water. When Moriah finds out he's living nearby, she is going to freak out."

"You mean, you haven't already told her?" Nicolas said.

"I was afraid she'd *never* come if she knew. If she ever did make it here, I was going to let her get acclimated to all the strangeness of the village first and introduce her to the people, and then after a few days break it to her really gently."

"You think Karyona and Fusiwe won't break it to her gently?"

"Fusiwe is too distracted by all his responsibilities, and Karyona might look sweet and gentle, but she's a bulldog once she gets an idea in her head. Without me there, I'm afraid she'll try to get Moriah to go with her. That would be a disaster."

"I tried to keep her from coming," Nicolas said.

"I don't blame you. I can hardly believe she did!"

"She thought you were dying," Nicolas said. "And she loves you. I have to admit, the girl has grit. The helicopter ride was especially terrifying, but she endured it."

"Just like that?" Ben said. "She just sat there and endured everything?"

"No," Nicolas smiled. "I'm pretty sure I'll be getting a cleaning bill from the company that owns the Leer jet. She almost made it to the bathroom in time, but her stomach didn't quite cooperate. Then, in the helicopter, she was more terrified than I have ever seen anyone in my life."

"But she made it."

"Yes, she made it."

"I need to get back there, Nicolas."

"As soon as you're strong enough. Kathy would never forgive me if I came all this way and didn't do my job."

"Is she pregnant?" Ben asked.

Nicolas was surprised. "Why do you ask?"

"Katherine would be here with you unless she was either sick or pregnant."

"You have a good understanding of people. We're expecting a little one in seven months. God is good."

"All the time." Ben closed his eyes and was sound asleep before Nicolas could say another word.

"Amen, my friend," Nicolas said, as he smoothed the red curls back from Ben's freckled face. "All the time."

Chapter Thirty-Three

The meal Karyona taught her how to fix was made up of a mixture containing manioc flour patted out and baked on hot stones into a flat bread. This was eaten with a sort of stew of chopped tapir meat along with fresh pineapple, which Karyona had also cut from her garden.

"We will wait until another time to prepare snake for you," Karyona teased. "That was hard for Violet to eat at first too, but she grew to like it."

None of this cooking was done alone. From the moment Karyona and Moriah harvested the manioc roots, they were accompanied by chattering, curious women and several children. They were a healthy people. The children had strong teeth and sturdy little bodies. Two of the little boys ran around with tiny homemade bows and arrows, competing with each other without much expertise. Several of the women wore vestiges of paint—perhaps left over from some small celebration for which they wanted to look nice.

The tight-knit relationships struck her as admirable. These women apparently spent nearly all day every day in one another's company and seemed to want to do so.

One elderly woman took a special interest in her. With no children to keep an eye on, she seemed to delight in teaching her how to do small tasks. She would demonstrate and then pantomime for Moriah to copy her actions. When Moriah did something well, the old woman would smile and nod in an exaggerated manner, as though encouraging a small child. She also pointed at objects and had Moriah repeat certain Yahnowa words as she pointed. It didn't take an expert in linguistics to know that the old woman was trying to teach her the names of the items.

She had seen not one store-bought article among them. What bits of clothing they wore were made out of plant fiber. The decorations they wore around their necks and in their hair were made up of shells, feathers, bone and more plant fibers—all brightly colored. She thought she understood why Ben's hut was so bare now. He must have decided to live with as few Western possessions as possible so as not to disturb this culture that had used only the things they could gather or make from the natural world for thousands of years.

Fusiwe came back from his dental work at the other village and found her working with the women.

"I have news," he said. "I stopped at Ben's hut and found a message on his computer."

"What does it say?" Moriah jumped up from where she had been sitting.

"I do not know." The weary tribesman shrugged. "I cannot yet read well."

She ran to the hut with Fusiwe and Karyona following close behind.

The message was from Nicolas; it had been there since yesterday and it was maddeningly short but held the most important information.

> *"If you get this—the Huey held together. We are at Sao Paulo hospital. Ben is alive. At this point, that is all we know."*

That evening, as she climbed back into Ben's bed and pulled the mosquito netting around her, she wondered what the future held. Would she soon be living here permanently? Would she learn to live with the heat, the dangers and the lack of privacy?

Or would the unthinkable happen. Would she end up accompanying Ben's body back home? Even though she now knew he was safely in the hospital, she could not erase the fact from her mind that two villagers had recently died from the same disease.

* * *

She did not sleep well that night. It was the heat and worry over Ben. There was also the sound of hungry mosquitos buzzing around outside the netting.

Worst of all, she kept replaying the sympathy that was in Karyona's voice as she described Moawa. She felt guilty for not accompanying her friend when she went to care for the old man. Then she felt angry over feeling guilty. She kept telling herself that he was not her responsibility. Moawa could starve to death out there for all she cared.

In the morning, another quick bath using yesterday's underwear as a wash cloth—less clumsy than the t-shirt. Maybe her underwear would be clean enough after it dried to use again. She was trying to be sparing with her clean clothes because she had no idea how long she would be here. Another protein bar was washed down by tepid water.

This time she did not wait for Karyona to come to her, but walked into the circle of Yahnowa huts looking for her friend. She found her cooking pieces of fish over a small fire using only green twigs as a sort of grill.

"I didn't know you could do that," Moriah said, fascinated.

"Sometimes the sticks catch fire and we lose some meat," Karyona said. "But fish cook so fast there is little danger."

"Do you need any help today?" Moriah asked.

"I am making this fish as part of Moawa's morning meal," Karyona said. "It would be nice if I had some company when I take it to him. Last night it was difficult."

"What made it so difficult?"

"It is always hard for me to go to see him. He sits in the hut Ben and Rashawe built and waits for someone to bring him food and water. Having someone to talk to for a few minutes seems even more important to him than the food we bring. One of the saddest things is that he is so hungry to talk each time we come. He asks about the men; what they have brought home from the hunt. He asks if there have been any new children born. Anything to make me stay a bit longer."

"But he is alive," Moriah said. "Which is more than I can say for my parents."

"He knows what he did, and is grateful to be cared for at all," Karyona said. "But we are a people used to living together. We are seldom alone. We don't want to be alone. It is not in our culture to live apart like he is being made to do."

"Why did his village reject him?"

"They think he brought illness and bad luck into their village."

"Did he?"

"I don't know. Last night I ran out of things to tell him and so I told him about you being in the village."

"I wish you hadn't." Moriah suddenly had a sick feeling in the pit of her stomach. "What did he say?"

"He asked to see you."

Oh goodness. Would her friend *never* stop pestering her with this?

"I can't, Karyona," she said. "Please don't keep asking. I just can't."

In her own, sweet, gentle way, Karyona was relentless. "But you need to do this."

"No," Moriah said. "I don't. It is not within me to do what you want me to."

"You are not telling the truth," Karyona said, in a matter-of-fact voice. "You can do this. You can go talk to an old man."

Moriah was silent. What was it that Crystal had said? Something about asking if she thought Moawa would look the same after all these years, if seeing him might help?

"It would be a kindness for you to go talk to him," Karyona said. "And it would make Ben so happy and proud of you."

"How do you know it would make Ben happy and proud of me?"

"Because we talked about it. Ben said you were strong and kind. He said he thought you would be able to do this... eventually."

"You aren't going to let up until I go, are you?"

"Probably not." Karyona gently lifted the fish onto a clean banana leaf and expertly wrapped it into a neat package.

Chapter Thirty-Four

How is Ben?" Matt asked, as he entered the hospital room.

"He's getting crankier," Nicolas said.

"I'm not cranky," Ben said, irritably. "I just want to get out of here."

"He wants to get back to the village," Nicolas said. "I'm afraid he'll try to escape if I turn my back on him."

"He'll have to walk then," Matt said. "Dad's still trying to get the Huey patched up."

"Is that even possible?" Nicolas asked.

"I'm not sure. The other mechanics at the airfield are still scratching their heads over how we even made it back. What with the damaged blades, the damaged hydraulic line and only a few drops of fuel left in the fuel line—some of them are calling it a miracle flight. Dad's eating it up."

"Your dad has both faith and courage," Nicolas said. "That's a great combination for a missions pilot."

"Yes," Matt said, fondly. "My dad is also a little bit crazy."

* * *

Another day passed, and Nicolas had sent a message that the doctors said Ben was passed the worst and was slowly gaining strength. That eased her mind greatly.

Now that worry over Ben had eased, the thought of Moawa being only a short walk through the forest began to crowd out everything else in her head.

Cowering inside Ben's hut until she could escape back to Canada wasn't much of an option. Especially since Karyona and her own conscience was apparently not going to give her any peace until she went to see the old man.

Deep down, choosing to face him had little to do with Karyona and everything to do with the fact that she was being given an opportunity to neutralize her last great fear. She had a strong feeling that she would never be completely healed of the trauma of the past until she could face the man who had been the root cause of all of it.

She had conquered the bridge. She'd conquered her fear of flying... sort of. She could conquer this final challenge. Chief Moawa was old and blind, she reassured herself. He could no longer hurt her.

It's like ripping off a band aid, she told herself. Go to his hut. Say whatever it is that Karyona wants you to say. Get it over with and get out. Five minutes max, she told herself. She could bear anything for five minutes.

Put like that, it didn't sound so hard. Except that it was. It was very hard.

"Time to get a backbone, Moriah," she said out loud.

Stiffening her spine and squaring her shoulders, she left Ben's hut and walked to Karyona and Fusiwe's hut where Karyona was grilling another piece of fish over a small fire.

"Okay. I'm ready," she told Karyona.

"Ready for what?" Karyona said.

"Isn't this the time you usually take Moawa's breakfast to him?

"Yes. I am preparing it now."

"I'll go with you."

Karyona glanced up and a slow smile spread across her face. "I am pleased." She quickly gathered Moawa's food together and stood.

"The path is narrow. Stay directly behind me... and please don't touch anything."

In spite of what lay ahead, Moriah smiled inwardly at Karyona's admonition. She vowed that if she lived here, she would make it her business to learn every tree, plant, insect and animal so she would know which ones were dangerous and those that were not.

People had survived in this rainforest for years. They'd given birth, hunted, grown gardens, laughed and told stories. It *must* be possible to live here safely once one learned how to deal with the environment.

Carefully, she followed her friend through the jungle upon a narrow path that had seen but little foot traffic. Karyona carried a wooden bowl filled with what appeared to be a sort of porridge made of manioc in addition to the package of fish. In a small clearing, a tiny, ragged, hut sat utterly alone.

Her first thought was that it would be dangerous to live out so far from everyone. He wouldn't be able to protect himself from any sort of predator, or know if a poisonous snake had slithered into the hut. He wouldn't be able to call for help if he fell and hurt himself or got sick.

She hardened herself. The punishment was harsh, but he deserved it.

Moriah could feel her heart pounding harder the closer she got to the hut. Her feet began to drag as she forced herself forward. Every step felt as though she were pushing through quicksand. This was a familiar feeling—something she'd experienced repeatedly while crossing the bridge at Little Current.

Karyona stopped several feet from the hut and called out.

A frail voice answered in Yahnowa from within.

It became difficult to breathe.

Her friend politely motioned for Moriah to enter before her. Moriah shook her head, refusing. A memory of gruesome images flashed through her mind.

Karyona entered.

Moriah stared at the opening of the hut. If there was one thing she had learned during her work with Crystal, it was the value of pushing her way past the fear.

Almost in a trance, forcing herself to take each individual step, she made herself move toward the door of the hut. She stood there taking deep breaths as she reminded the little girl within that this old man could no longer hurt her. Then she ducked her head and entered. Once inside, it took a moment for her eyes to adjust to the dim interior of the hut. What she saw was disturbing.

An old man huddled on the ground with his back against the circular wall. The interior of the hut was nearly bare except for a hammock attached to the poles at the top.

Karyona spoke softly to Moawa as she offered him the bowl of porridge and then opened the package of fish which she spread out upon the ground. He reached eager hands out to her and grasped the wooden bowl. His clouded eyes stared straight ahead as he hungrily fed himself by scooping the porridge into his mouth with his fingers. The bowl was quickly emptied. Karyona took it from him, sat it aside, then grasped his hand and gently led it to the pieces of fish lying beside him. He smiled widely after tasting the fish, and murmured something to Karyona that Moriah assumed was the Yahnowa equivalent of thank-you.

Moriah stood rooted to the spot, directly in front of the door, struggling to equate this frail, blind man with her parents' killer. How could this be the man she remembered? This shrunken old man could not possibly be Moawa. There were no similarities at all.

After he had finished the fish, Karyona removed a hollow gourd from a peg, dipped it into a container of water in a corner, and handed it to him. After he had drunk deeply and noisily, Karyona spoke to him again at some length, glancing from time to time at Moriah.

His face lost the look of pleasure he had worn while eating his simple meal. He grew sober, his head lifted and it seemed as though he was looking straight at her even though he was obviously blind. Then he spoke and Karyona translated.

"He asks if I am completely certain that you are the little girl who got away."

"Tell him that I am. Say that I still hold the memories of him killing my mother and father," Moriah said. "Tell him I survived only because of the courage of your father and brother."

Karyona translated, then listened carefully to his reply. She questioned him again, as though clarifying his answer.

"He says you did not get away. He says he let you go."

"Really?" A laugh of disbelief burst from her lips. "I seriously doubt that."

Moawa spoke a few more words as though he understood what Moriah had said.

"No," Karyona said. "He did let you go. He says he and his men tracked my father and brother planning to kill all of you. They caught up with you when you were crossing the long rope bridge at the big waterfall. He says my father was at the midway point when Moawa called his men off."

Moriah was shocked. "Why didn't he kill us?"

Karyona spoke with the old man a few more moments and then translated.

"He says it was because you cried out so pitifully. Moawa says it reminded him of his son's cries the first time Moawa carried him across. His son had been about your age."

"His son?"

"The one Nicolas' mother could not save."

"What are you talking about?"

"Oh? I thought you knew. Moawa's son developed gangrene after breaking both his legs in a bad fall. Moawa carried him to the missionary clinic, hoping the good doctor could save his life."

"And she couldn't." Moriah voice was dull.

"It was too late. He died here. Moawa didn't understand. He believed the people at the clinic had deliberately killed him. He blamed himself for not trusting the Shaman, for trusting his son's life to Western medicine."

The old man spoke again. Moriah didn't understand the words, but she heard the sound of regret in his voice.

Yet again, Karyona translated.

"Moawa says he was crazy with grief and anger at the death of his only son. He knew only revenge killing and so he killed."

Moriah rubbed her hand across her face. The knowledge that Moawa had killed out of misdirected grief was a revelation. She had experienced enough of grief herself to have some idea of the control it could have over someone's emotions.

"Tell him it was an evil thing he did."

Karyona spoke softly, listened and then turned back to Moriah. "He says he knows that. He says that he and his people suffered much because of his actions."

Moriah had come here out of duty to Ben and friendship to Karyona. She had come to overcome her fear, to prove to herself that she was brave enough to face anything, even her parents' killer.

Now, to her surprise, she felt her heart softening toward the old man. This was not something she wanted to happen. She had not come with the intention of forgiving him. It had never even occurred to her that she could.

Deliberately, she tried to harden her heart against him. "Tell him I hate him."

Karyona glanced up at her friend, shocked. "I won't!"

"Then tell him I've been a prisoner on an island for twenty years because of the damage he did. Tell him he nearly destroyed three families."

Karyona sat back on her heels, gave it some thought and then began to translate.

The old man interrupted her, his voice cracking with emotion.

Karyona's gentle eyes filled with sadness. "He says he knows. He wants you to forgive him."

Moriah looked at the sad old man sitting in the dirt, heard the pain in his voice and felt her heart shatter.

The old man waited in silence.

Moriah stumbled back out the door, her body shaking, her chest heaving, her thoughts tumbling wildly.

She had overcome so much. Wasn't it enough? Did she *have* to forgive him?

That was not possible.

A child's two-year silence.

A family torn apart.

Nightmares. Wet beds. Terror...

She paced back and forth in front of the hut, fighting with herself. Fighting the desire to start running and not stop. Away from this hut, this man, Karyona, the village, the heat, the danger. When Ron came back she was going to climb on that helicopter and get out of this place. She'd been a fool to come, regardless of Ben's illness. She suddenly craved the crisp, pure, lake air flowing over her beloved island instead of the smothering humidity of this place. Homesickness flooded her.

The suddenly, instead of Manitoulin Island, a different image flooded into her mind. That of a man forgiving his murderers even while he hung dying on a cross.

Who was she to do less?

This pitiful old man was no monster. He never had been. He was nothing more than a father who had lost a son, and who had lashed out against the foreigners whom he believed to be responsible.

Once again, she entered Moawa's dimly-lit hut.

Three steps in, she felt her legs give way and she fell to her knees onto the dirt floor of the poor hut, her bitterness draining away from her broken heart, her head bowed in submission.

"Tell him that I understand, and I forgive him."

Karyona spoke to Moawa. His face creased into a smile. He stretched his arm out into the space reaching out for something.

Moriah knew he was reaching out to touch her.

On her hands and knees, as though propelled by a force outside herself, she crawled the four remaining feet across the dirt floor between them and allowed him to lay his hand upon her head. He held it there, speaking with dignity and purpose. The years that he had led his village was in his voice.

"Moawa says for you not to grieve anymore," Karyona voice was choked with tears. "He says that he will be a father to you."

Chapter Thirty-Five

Ben strained to catch a glimpse of his village, but all he saw was an unbroken sea of treetops until the helicopter landed. He was disappointed that Moriah wasn't there to meet him in the tiny clearing.

Several of the village children ran to greet him, ducking under the blades of the borrowed helicopter despite Ron's shouts to stay away. As the blades ceased to rotate, Ben and Nicolas climbed out.

"Whoa." Nicolas reached out a hand to steady him when Ben swayed. "You aren't a hundred percent yet, friend, take it easy."

He did not want to take it easy. He wanted to see Moriah. He wanted to see with his own eyes that she had truly come to him.

Lying in the hospital bed with little to do except think, he had driven himself nearly mad with worry about what she would do when she learned of Moawa's presence near the village.

He had meant to tell her, of course. Eventually. When he got back to Manitoulin Island and when they were face to face so he could personally deal with the emotional fallout.

He had been so desperate to get back to her that Nicolas had become convinced he would heal more quickly in the village.

"I know you are anxious to see her," Nicolas shouldered his bag with one arm and assisted Ben with the other, "but Fusiwe saved your life. Don't neglect to thank him."

Ben was so weak, the children nearly pulled him down as they clung to him in their happiness at having him back. While Nicolas shooed them away, Fusiwe walked toward him, hand extended.

Ben ignored Fusiwe's Western gesture and pulled him into a close embrace. "Thank you, my friend. Thank you for saving me."

"It was nothing," Fusiwe said, modestly.

"If you hadn't figured out how to work the computer and send a message, I would be dead by now—not to mention keeping my fever down until Nicolas could get here."

"Karyona and Rashawe helped with the fever, but I worked the computer," Fusiwe said, with some pride.

"How did you know what to do?"

"I watched you."

"I should have thought to teach you. I'm sorry, Fusiwe. I didn't know you were interested."

"I am very interested."

"Then as soon as I get settled, I'll teach you more." Ben glanced around, "Is Moriah alright? Why isn't she here?"

"Little Green Eyes is too busy to come." Fusiwe grinned, as though holding back a secret.

"Doing what?"

"Fixing things."

"I know she likes to fix things... but *here*?"

"Come see."

Fusiwe placed Ben's arm around his shoulder, taking over the job of supporting him from Nicolas as the four men made their way through the jungle.

Ben's first glimpse of Moriah astonished him. It was definitely Moriah, and she was most definitely busy. Busy building a new hut. She stood, holding a crossbeam of lashed bamboo above her head, while two of the village men secured it to supports they'd dug into the ground.

From what he could tell, she had somehow managed to improve slightly on the design.

"Hello, Ben." She grinned at him mischievously when she saw him "Good to see you again. Nice day, isn't it."

Her hair was in a ponytail and she had a blue handkerchief tied around her forehead. Her white t-shirt was stained with sweat, her khaki pants were smudged with dirt. Her arms were stretched above her head grasping the bamboo and her face was flushed with the effort.

She was the most gorgeous creature he had ever seen.

"I see you found a way to keep yourself busy while I was gone."

"Oh you know me," Moriah said. "Always looking for a project."

They both burst out laughing at their absurd commonplace tone, as well as the sheer delight of being able to once again be together.

He wanted to run, grab her, twirl her around and kiss her senseless. Unfortunately, he could barely stand alone. It also appeared that, even if he were strong enough to do so, the structure she was supporting would collapse if she let go.

"Want to explain what you're doing?" he asked.

"Well, I seem to have gotten myself adopted while you were away."

"Adopted?"

"Yep. I'm building a home for the newest member of our family."

As happy as he was to see Moriah, and as badly as he wanted to hear this, his legs felt like they were quickly turning to rubber.

Rashawe came running out of Ben's hut with his chair and Ben gratefully collapsed onto it.

"Thank you," Ben gasped. "I'm weaker than I knew. Now, tell me, Moriah. For whom are you building this new home?"

"I had nothing to do with this." Fusiwe held his hands up and stepped away. "It was all Karyona and Moriah's idea."

Ben turned to Nicolas. "Do you know what they are talking about?"

"I've been at the hospital with *you*, remember?" Nicolas said. "Moriah, what are you up to? Wasn't Ben's hut big enough?"

A familiar voice quavered in Yahnowa from behind Moriah.

Ben was startled at the sound.

Moawa shuffled into view, supported by a rough stick, led by one of the children.

"Uh, Moriah, honey?" Ben said. "Do you know who that is?"

"Yes." Moriah was finally free to release the crossbeam. She scooted out from beneath it, brushed her hands on her pants, then ran over and gave Ben a kiss. "I know exactly who he is and I know who he was. I also know why he did what he did. I'm building this new hut for him."

"Why?"

Moriah glanced meaningfully at the villagers crowding in around them, eavesdropping as Karyona translated every word.

"He asked my forgiveness and I gave it. Then he offered himself in place of my father whom he killed. I accepted that offer."

Who *was* this woman! Apparently she was not the same person he had carried sobbing off the Little Current bridge. "I'm impressed. But why the hut?"

"Oh that. He shouldn't be out there in the bush by himself, Ben. He's old and blind. He needs to be close where we can take care of him." Moriah walked over to where Moawa stood, placed one hand on his shoulder and glanced around at the people as though daring them to argue with her. "Family should take care of family."

Ben felt tears sting his eyes. In all she had done, in all she had overcome, he had never been prouder.

Moawa stood up straight as Karyona translated Moriah's last sentence. He lifted his chin as though challenging anyone to question his right to live within the village. No one did.

Moriah untied the handkerchief and wiped the sweat from her face.

"You need to excuse me now, Ben. I can't talk any longer. I was hoping to get this finished and Moawa moved in by nightfall."

Nicolas had quietly watched the entire scene from behind Ben's chair.

"So." Nicolas' voice was emotionless as they watched Moriah go back to work. "The man who murdered my mother is now to be considered some sort of an in-law?"

"Apparently so," Ben said.

"Interesting." Nicolas was quiet for a while as they watched Moriah work. "Hatred is a heavy thing to carry."

"I've found it to be so."

Nicolas sighed. "I suppose if Moriah can forgive this man, I shall try to as well. She's the one who has suffered the most."

"We all suffered from his actions, Nicolas. But no longer, by the grace of God, no longer."

Nicolas cleared his throat. "We need to get you to bed now. You've done enough for one day."

"Nicolas?"

"Yes?"

"Thank-you buying the lighthouse. Thank-you for saving my life. Thank-you for bringing the four of us together so we can help heal one another."

"I am a selfish man, Ben. I bought the lighthouse solely as an excuse to be close to Katherine. I hired you because you were a skilled stonemason and available. I saved your life because that's what doctors do. I never expected any of the rest of this to happen. It never once crossed my mind."

"A selfish man wouldn't have put his own life in danger to save a missionary's life," Ben said. "A selfish man couldn't possibly love Katherine as whole-heartedly as you do. But I believe you when you say you never expected any of this to happen. God used you, my friend."

"I would be pleased to believe that." Nicolas steered Ben toward his hut. "Come. You need to rest."

Reluctantly, Ben allowed Nicolas to tuck him into his sleeping platform. Exhaustion soon overtook him and he fell asleep listening to the unbelievable sound of Moriah building a hut for Chief Moawa.

* * *

"Ben?" Moriah whispered.

He awoke with a start.

"Everything is alright," she reassured him. "It's me."

"Did you finish the hut?" Ben said.

She sat on the platform and he wrapped one arm around her waist, loving the feel of her. So many times he had dreamed of this. It was hard to believe she was here and real. Living, breathing—and smelling like she had done a hard day's work in the tropics. Yep, she was real, alright.

"I have a little more to do in the morning, but it's mostly finished."

"Never, in my wildest dreams did I ever think you would react this way to Moawa."

"Neither did I."

"Why did you?"

Moriah hesitated. "One minute I was so filled with hatred I could barely breathe. The next minute, my heart was in pieces and all I could feel was compassion for him. It's hard to explain."

"I know. I went through a similar experience when I found him."

"It felt as though God, himself, touched my heart."

"Maybe that's because He did."

"You felt it too?"

"I couldn't have forgiven Moawa on my own. I loved my father too,

Moriah." He gently tweaked her nose. "But you didn't have to adopt the man, babe."

"He adopted *me*. At least that's the way I remember it. He's no monster, Ben. He's just a sad old man. Karyona said that, since I've chosen to adopt him, the rest of the village will accept him too. Building the hut for him is sort of a visible symbol to them."

"And besides that, you're enjoying it."

"I am. Is there any rule that says a missionary wife can't build?"

"Honey, you can swing from the vines and sing *Zippity Doo Dah* for all I care. Just as long as you'll stay with me. I'm afraid you'll leave now that I'm better."

"Why would I leave?"

"I don't know. To prepare for that wedding in the lighthouse? Wasn't I supposed to fly up there?"

"Well, about that wedding…" She pulled her feet onto the platform and hugged her knees to her chest. "…is having that lighthouse wedding really important to you?"

"No. I just want be married to you. It doesn't matter to me how we get there."

"I talked to Ron. He said he can fly a preacher in when he comes to pick up Nicolas. I hope I'm not being too pushy."

"Moriah. Please. Be my guest. Be pushy."

She smiled and gave him a quick kiss. "Good. You rest. I'll take care of everything."

Chapter Thirty-Six

"Are you finished yet?" Moriah winced as Karyona sectioned off yet another hank of hair.

"Almost." Karyona braided it tightly. "Now, you're all done. Stand up and let me see you."

Moriah stood. She was wearing a white tank top, khaki shorts... and a skirt made of some sort of dried grass she couldn't identify. Her hair was braided and bedecked with flowers, *and* she was wearing paint.

Karyona had carefully explained that, although traditionally, the Yahnowa didn't have any sort of formal wedding ceremonies, they considered it rude to attend special occasions without painting themselves. Even paying a friendly visit to a neighboring tribe involved an elaborate ritual of body painting. Moriah supposed that, for a people with few clothes, it was their answer to formal dress. Karyona and Fusiwe were no exception. Not only had they painted themselves with festive colors, Karyona had insisted on beautifying Moriah as well.

Moriah knew that to Western eyes she looked a sight, but Karyona was so excited about preparing her for her wedding, she couldn't hurt her childhood friend by refusing. Still, she was a little relieved there was no mirror in which to see her reflection.

With longing, she remembered the lovely, long white wedding gown hanging in her closet. It was four thousand miles away and completely inappropriate for this jungle village. Moriah tried to find humor in her predicament, in spite of cringing inwardly a little at the thought of going to Ben as a bride in such a garb.

Chopper blades sounded in the distance, hopefully indicating Ron bringing in the preacher. Karyona glanced outside. "It's nearly time," she said. Then she looked again. "Oh! My mother and father are home. I'm so glad. I sent one of the young men to find them and to tell them you were here."

Moriah peeked around Karyona and saw a familiar-looking middle-aged Yahnowa couple walking toward her. Akawe proudly carried a wooden chest.

"I think my mother and father are bringing you a gift," Karyona said.

Akawe's expression was serious as he approached Moriah and ceremoniously laid the wooden chest at her feet.

Napognuma then knelt, opened the lid and lifted out a bundle wrapped in cloth and handed it to her. She carefully unfolded the fabric. In her hands lay a cracked, cheap, white leather Bible. She handed it to Moriah. On the front, printed in fading gold letters, was the name "Mary Ann Robertson."

"It's my mother's!"

Napognuma spoke and Karyona translated.

"Your mother left her Bible in our hut the night she brought you to stay. It was the only thing of hers not consumed by the fire. My mother has cared for it all this time. Now, she wants you to have it on your wedding day."

Moriah opened the onionskin pages. They still smelled faintly of strawberries, her mother's favorite scent. A thin sachet lay pressed between the pages.

For twenty years a woman had guarded another woman's Bible—which she could not read. Moriah felt like weeping at the lack of thought and importance she had once given to Ben's work.

"I don't know if I should accept this, Karyona. How great of a sacrifice is it to your parents?"

"Probably even greater than you know. It has been a treasure in our home. If you are uncomfortable receiving it, perhaps you could carry it with you for your wedding and then give it to my mother for safekeeping? For so many years, when she was sick or frightened, she would hold it and pray."

"Then, of course I'll give it back. Please tell your mother my intentions along with my heartfelt thanks."

Karyona did, and Moriah saw a look of relief come over Napognuma's face. Although older, it was the same sweet face that had cradled and protected her on the worst night of her life.

Akawe smiled now and held out his arms. Moriah was shocked to find herself flying into them. He had put his life at great risk to save a little white girl. Akawe patted her on the shoulder. "Safe," he said. "Safe."

The village buzzed with excitement when Moriah emerged from the doorway of Karyona's hut. Ben glanced at her, raised his eyebrows and a grin slowly spread across his face.

Moawa waited nearby. She had told him that, in her country, fathers walked their daughters to their husbands-to-be and then gave them away. Moawa said that he thought this was a barbarous practice and carefully explained that there should be some sort of goods exchanged for her. She agreed wholeheartedly.

Ben, in deference to his new father-in-law, respectfully gave Moawa a small pouch of Canadian coins that Moawa carefully counted, then tied the pouch around his neck.

Now, she took the old headman's arm and they slowly proceeded toward Ben. Moawa supported himself on a new cane she had made for him.

Moriah could tell the minister was struggling not to gape. Nicolas had given up the struggle and merely stared with his mouth open. Neither of the men mattered. The only person that mattered was Ben, who looked at her, in spite of her odd dress and paint, as though he couldn't wait to spend the rest of his life with her.

"Gentlemen," Moriah said when she and Moawa arrived in front of Ben and the minister. "I believe we're ready."

* * *

Later that night, Moriah and Ben lay beside each other in his hut, nearly paralyzed with giggles.

"I wish I'd had a camera," Ben said.

"To take a picture of your lovely bride?"

"No, to take a picture of Nicolas. I was afraid a bird would fly into his mouth and make a nest."

"I thought the old headman was a nice touch."

"He lent our marriage dignity," Ben agreed.

"Do you suppose we're truly married?"

"*That*, I can assure you, is one thing I'm absolutely certain of. Rick Carver is a bonafide Baptist minister and the marriage certificate he brought is as official as it comes. Rick said he would register it for us as soon as he got back to Sao Paulo."

She turned on her side and stroked Ben's face. "I'm so glad you're back here with me, but I wouldn't have missed the past few days here for the world."

"Life does get interesting along the Amazon."

"I have a feeling that life with you is going to be interesting no matter where we are."

"I'm proud of you, you know." Ben drew her close.

"In what way?"

"Pretty much everything. The way you fought to come here. The gift of forgiveness you gave to Moawa. How you managed to look regal in a grass skirt and with your hair sticking out all over your head."

"We're going to have a good life, Ben."

"That we are."

She snuggled her head against his neck. "I saw Nicolas give you an envelope before he left with Ron. Did you open it?"

"Forgot all about it. He said it was a wedding gift. It's over there beneath the lantern if you want to look."

Moriah went to the table and pulled the envelope out from under the lantern.

She didn't think Nicolas would have given them money. Currency was pretty much unusable this far in the jungle.

What she saw when she opened the envelope nearly made her heart stop.

"You aren't going to believe this, Ben. "

"What am I not going to believe?"

"It's a letter. Here, you read it out loud. I'm not entirely certain I saw what I think I did."

Ben sat up and took the letter out of her hand.

Dear Moriah,

I know you've never liked me and I don't blame you. I don't deserve Katherine or you and I probably never will. But I am aware that the real reason you and I got off on the wrong foot was my purchase of the lighthouse. You are right. The lighthouse belongs to you, in spirit if not in deed. You are the one who's loved it, cared for it, tried to protect it, and finally restored it. It should belong to you.

Fortunately, I have no need for it anymore. I have, instead, a life with Katherine, which is all I ever wanted in the first place. When I get back to Canada, I will have my attorney draw up a deed, which will put the lighthouse in your name. You and Ben will need a home whenever you are between mission trips and although you will always be welcome in the lodge with us, as your family grows, you might want a place like the lighthouse to which you can come.

I know I am sometimes stiff and awkward with words, and that is why I am writing this instead of saying it. Moawa has already claimed you for a daughter here in the Southern Hemisphere, but if you're willing, even though I'm twenty years late, I would like to claim you as a daughter in the North.

Sincerely,

Nicolas Bennett, MD.

Both Moriah and Ben sat in stunned silence as several seconds ticked by.

"Should we allow him to do that?" he asked.

"I don't know," Moriah answered, slowly. "But a big part of me is wanting to yell 'Yippie!' right now."

"It's your decision."

Moriah tapped her chin with the letter, considering. "Then it's my lighthouse. I'll make him the best northern daughter he ever dreamed of. That is, if he treats Katherine right. She's pregnant, you know."

"Nicolas told me. That's such good news. She's always wanted a baby of her own."

"Did she tell you that?"

"No. I saw it in her face when she held Camelia's newborn."

Moriah folded Nicolas' letter, placed it carefully in the envelope and put it back beneath the lamp. Then she blew out the lamp and padded across the floor to Ben, who lifted a sheet for her to crawl beneath. She adjusted the mosquito netting so it covered them both.

"How far along is Katherine?" Ben asked.

"Barely six weeks, why?"

"If something were to happen tonight…"

"Don't even say it." Moriah shut him up with a kiss. "I refuse to be pregnant the same time as Katherine. That's just way too weird."

Chapter Thirty-Seven

....

Manitoulin Island, Robertson Lighthouse

From far away, Moriah heard the cry of a child. She opened her eyes and saw Ben holding a naked newborn with a fuzzy head of red hair.

Their son.

Ben was sobbing so hard with happiness and relief, she was almost afraid he might drop the tiny, purplish infant. Fortunately, his hands were so large, the baby was securely cradled in them.

"Push again, dear," Katherine said, calmly.

Moriah summoned the strength to push once more, felt the release of afterbirth and collapsed back onto the pillows Ben had stacked behind her.

"Is he alright?" She felt herself slowly coming back from the private, primitive place she had gone while she had fought her way through the birth.

"Perfect," Katherine said. "And you didn't tear. You'll have an easy recovery."

"I had a good doctor and midwife," Moriah said, as Katherine kneaded her now empty abdomen.

"Don't cry, Petey, Daddy's here," Ben crooned to the furious newborn.

"Petey?" Katherine asked. "Where did that come from?"

"It's a McCain tradition, we alternate between three first names."

Ben shrugged. "Petras, Ebenezer and Peter. It's a stonemason thing."

"How so?"

"Both Peter and Petras means rock."

"And Ebenezer?

"Ebenezer means 'stone of help'."

Moriah gazed at her stalwart husband with loving eyes. "Ebenezer means 'stone of help'? You never told me that."

"It's not important."

"It fits you."

Katherine laid a blue receiving blanket on the bed. Ben placed the baby in the middle of it and stood back while Katherine turned his son into a sort of blue flannel burrito and placed him back in Ben's arms. Then she deftly bound Moriah with soft cloth, and helped her prop herself up to nurse her son. He was a hearty little guy and latched on as he had been programmed to do from time before time. Moriah smiled contentedly at his greed.

"Not too long this first time," Katherine said, after a few minutes. "I don't want you to get sore. Those little newborn tongues can be rougher than you realize."

"Can I hold him again?" Ben said, reaching out his arms. "I can hardly believe he's really ours."

"Sorry if I hurt you," Moriah noticed red marks on his arm and was fairly certain she'd put them there. "I didn't mean to."

"Hurt me?" Ben laughed. "You mean digging your fingernails into my bicep with one hand and nearly pulling a hank of hair out of my head with the other?" Ben said. "That was nothing. Piece of cake, lass. Totally worth it."

Katherine set a tall glass of water on the bedside table. "You'll need to drink a lot of this if you are going to nurse that baby."

"I'm thirsty already," Moriah said. "Thanks."

"I want to go tell Nicolas the good news, and I want to introduce Petey to his new little cousin," Ben said. "I'll be right back."

* * *

"It's over?" In the adjoining room, Nicolas sat holding a small bundle of his own in the crook of his arm. He had remained close by so that he could take over if Katherine needed him, but had chosen to give Moriah her privacy as long as everything was going well.

Ben carefully pulled the receiving blanket away from his sleeping son's face. "We have a healthy little boy. His name is Peter Jacob."

"I'm happy for you," Nicolas said. "Another boy. Isn't that something? We are rich men, McCain, with these sons to raise."

"Your Lucas David and our Peter Jacob are going to have a lot of fun together in a few years."

"You planning on sticking around for a while?"

"For a while. At least until Moriah recuperates and the baby stabilizes. Plus, she wants me to carve out a special stone before we leave,"

"What for?"

"To put in front of the lighthouse. It's to say, 'Robertson Lighthouse—In memory of Dr. Rachel Bennett, Petras McCain, Mary Ann and Jacob Robertson."

"They would like that, I think, especially now that you're using this place as a respite for missionaries."

"How many have come now for sabbaticals?"

"Check it out." Nicolas nodded toward a table. "The guestbook is right over there."

Ben opened a massive leather-bound book Katherine had found that resembled the old logbooks kept by the original light keepers. He turned to the first page. Five different ministers' families from around the world had enjoyed a no-cost, much-needed vacation here in the past nine months.

"It is a good use of this place," Nicolas said. "I'm glad you thought of it. They were all so grateful."

The sound of a pickup truck coming up the lighthouse road filtered in through the open window

"Who do you suppose that is?" Nicolas said. "Moriah certainly isn't up to company."

"Looks like Sam Black Hawk's truck." Ben opened the door as Sam scrambled out of his truck.

"Did Moriah have that baby yet?" Sam asked.

"About a half-hour ago."

"I figured. Heard she was in labor."

"How did you know?" Ben asked.

"Smoke signals." Sam caught sight of the infant in Ben's arms. "Well, would you look at that! Boy or girl?"

"Boy."

"Poor little fellow," Sam stroked the silky red fuzz on the baby's head. "Ugly little thing. Too bad he took after his daddy."

"I wouldn't let Moriah hear that if I were you." Ben laughed. "She thinks me and the baby are gorgeous."

"There's a baby present out in my truck for her, but I need help lifting it out."

"What kind of baby present is that heavy?"

"One she's going to love. You'll see. Better hand off your son to someone else and give me a hand."

Ben took the baby back to the bedroom. Moriah was sitting up in bed and eagerly held out her arms.

Ben laid the sleeping Petey in her arms and watched as she cradled him.

"Oh, Ben!" she said. "Isn't he the prettiest little thing? Can you even believe how beautiful he is?"

"Absolutely," Ben said. "I'll be right back."

He joined Sam and Nicolas out at the truck, curious as to what sort of baby present would require two men to carry it.

Then he saw it. Gleaming in the sun. Cushioned in layer after layer of pillows and blankets. Sparkling like a diamond.

"I drove five miles an hour all the way," Black Hawk said. "Took forever. Didn't think I'd ever get here, but I had to be careful."

"Your timing is perfect," Ben said. He was awestruck at his first look at a Fresnel lens. "You're right. Moriah is going to love this. You couldn't have possibly brought her anything she would appreciate more."

"I know," Black Hawk said. "That's why I brought it back."

Together, they carried the giant prism into the cottage while Nicolas held the outer door open for them.

While Ben and Black Hawk waited, Nicolas knocked at the door leading into the bedroom where Moriah lay.

"Katherine? Moriah has a visitor. Is it okay to come in?"

Katherine opened the door. "A visitor? Of course not…" The look of annoyance on her face turned into a look of wonder.

"Oh, Moriah. You aren't going to believe this." Katherine backed into the room as Ben and Black Hawk carried the gift to the foot of Moriah's bed.

Moriah glanced up from adoring her baby, her expression changing from maternal softness to astonished delight.

"It can't be! It was stolen!"

"You're right about that. I'm the one who stole it," Black Hawk said. "It was the only way I knew to make certain it was safe."

The Fresnel lens, over four-feet tall, every prism of glass polished to a diamond-like gleam, caught a beam of sunlight. Color spread across the bed, covering Moriah and her child in a rainbow.

Moriah caught her breath at the beauty. The baby turned his head toward it and blinked.

"This was the light your great-great-great-grandmother kept, little Petey," Moriah said. "We'll put it in the tower and someday you can help me light it for the ships out on the lake."

She looked at Sam Black Hawk who stood beaming at her from the foot of the bed. "How can I ever thank you, Sam?"

"I've already got that figured out. Can I be the one who strikes the first match to light the lamp the first time we fire this thing up?"

"Absolutely." Moriah turned to Ben. "Do you think it will be terribly difficult to install it, Ben?"

"Probably," Ben said. "But difficult things are what we do, isn't it?"

A look of understanding passed between them.

"Yes, my love," Moriah said, kissing the downy head of her newborn son. "That is exactly what we do."

Chapter Thirty-Eight

Wearing nothing but pajama bottoms, Ben paced the floor of the lighthouse cottage with their tiny, squalling bundle of joy. Moriah had tried to comfort the child until she was exhausted. Petey did not want to nurse, did not need new diapers, did not seem to be ill, but he was definitely not happy. Nor was he interested in going to sleep.

The baby honeymoon they had experience filled with awe and excitement had waned somewhat. It was amazing how a tiny scrap of humanity could show up and completely take over two people's lives. Unless he missed his guess, Petey was not going to go down tonight without a fight.

With a sigh, Ben gave up pacing, laid the baby on the couch while he squalled and began wrapping the stretchy material around himself that Moriah often used to carry the baby. It was only a long length of stretchy fabric, but it involved an intricate wrapping procedure that he was only now getting the hang of.

With Petey pitching a red-faced fit on the couch, tiny feet kicking and little fists waving, Ben finally got the wrap securely tied, picked up the furious infant and tucked him down inside the wrap. Then he began to walk in circles, singing in a low voice.

"A mighty fortress is our God.

A bulwark never failing..."

He didn't know any lullabies. His own bedtime songs, once his dad had gotten sober, had been hymns, so he figured that was about as good as any.

For variety, he sang the same verse in Yahnowa. Then Spanish and Portuguese. It was good practice for him, plus he thought maybe it would make learning languages a little easier for Petey when he got older. He thought the fact that Moriah had been exposed to Yahnowa at the age of five had made it a lot easier for her to pick up the language these past months. She had astonished the village as well as herself with her quick mastery. It was amazing how powerful things were that got imprinted early on a child's mind—both good and bad.

He caught sight of himself in a mirror and nearly laughed out loud. He was grateful for the privacy of the lighthouse cottage tonight. There was no one to see him marching around with his hair on end, looking about nine months pregnant with the baby tucked inside the wrap. It was attractive on Moriah, but it just looked silly on him.

Whether it was the feel of being against his daddy's bare chest, the womb-like security of the tight wrap, the comforting rumble of Ben's voice against his ear, or perhaps having already worn himself out crying, Petey finally fell asleep.

Ben stood still and took stock. With any luck, his son would sleep maybe as much as two hours before needing to nurse again. Moriah desperately needed sleep. And an excellent way to make certain Petey started crying again was to disturb his slumber by removing him from this wrap.

Therefore, the smartest thing to do was to stay awake, watch over the little fellow until he awoke hungry, and give Moriah a bit of time to recuperate.

He knew exactly what he wanted to do with the next two hours. Their lives had been quite topsy-turvy ever since they'd gotten home, but tonight might be a good time to begin translating the diary that the furniture refinisher had found in the old lighthouse desk.

Ben had already taken a look at it. Eliza's handwriting was as hard to read as everyone said. Especially since the ink had faded. So he had recently purchased an excellent magnifying glass.

With plenty of time to kill, he pulled a chair close to a table, sat out a fresh notebook and positioned a good lamp just so. Then, with Petey snug and content against his chest, he started to really examine the diary. Carefully, he thumbed his way through it all the way to the end. In the very back, inside of the back cover, he discovered a final and slightly more legible message written separately from the rest of the diary.

I am Eliza Robertson, a God-fearing woman. I am the third light keeper of the Tempest Bay lighthouse. Hard things happened within these walls. Let whoever finds this know that I did the best I could.

Author's Note

....

I was surprised to discover that during the 1800's and early 1900's, an era when it was taken for granted that a woman should be paid less than a man, over a hundred women kept the lights burning in lighthouses all over the United States and Canada. Most were women who were already familiar with the job, and who were granted the right to continue the work of their deceased husbands and fathers. They were given pay equal to their male counterparts long before women won the right to vote.

Many took on this hazardous job while also raising large families. Most impressive of all were the women who rowed out alone in storms to rescue those who would otherwise have perished.

Sometimes they faced starvation in the north when the ships that tended the lights could not break through the spring ice to bring provisions. They made hundreds of weary trips up staircases to carry fuel and supplies to keep the light burning. They went without sleep night after night to ensure the lights did not go out. They struggled with loneliness, danger, sickness, sleeplessness, and isolation while keeping those beacons of hope and guidance shining out upon the turbulent waters.

It is impossible to calculate the vast numbers of lives and ships they saved.

Modern day people love the romantic notions of lighthouses. The endurance and dedication of the old light keepers grabs the heart and excites the imagination. Many history buffs devote much of their lives to researching and preserving the lore and history of our remaining lighthouses.

As I researched this series of books, that fact created a problem for me as an author. I try to record the settings of my books as accurately as possible. In this case, it was my beloved Manitoulin Island that I wanted to describe. I did not think choosing an existing lighthouse as a backdrop for a fictional family was going to be well-received by those who have meticulously researched the struggles of the actual families who lived in specific lighthouses.

So, I made one up.

I chose the general location of Providence Bay (which I rename Tempest Bay) where a lighthouse once stood before it burned down. I took great license with the immediate area, creating a peninsula and nearby fishing resort that does not exist. The characters I put in the lighthouse were not based on anyone I know. Michael's Bay (which I rename Gabriel's Bay) is Manitoulin's only ghost town.

Lighthouses similar to the one I describe do exist, however. I chose to pattern Moriah's lighthouse after the Imperial Towers built around the Great Lakes in the early 1800's. They had the stonework that I needed for the story. I read extensively and visited Great Lakes lighthouses to be as accurate as possible in my descriptions. I apologize to lighthouse historians for any mistakes I might have made.

The Yahnowa tribe where Ben lives and works does not exist. However, I tried to make the customs, habits, and habitats as believable and accurate as possible based on my research into some of the larger Amazonian rainforest tribes. A warning, though. Studying the treatment of the indigenous tribes of the Amazon is heartbreaking.

The phobia with which Moriah struggles, does exist. My hope is that as we watch her battle against fear unfold, it might help us face our own demons with a bit more courage.

-Serena

My Heartfelt Thanks To:

Charlie Robertson, owner of the once-famous rock shop on Manitoulin Island. I appreciate the example you have been of choosing joy in spite of great loss.

Mamie (Coriell) Robertson, my transplanted cousin, who followed her heart to Manitoulin Island to be with Charlie. Thank you for telling us about the island so many years ago.

Wanda Whittington, Charlie's granddaughter. Thank you for patiently sharing your knowledge of your beloved Manitoulin Island with me and for your amazing hospitality.

My family, for taking the time to help me explore and research the island. The depth of your continued support and encouragement continues to astonish and humble me.

My church who so lovingly took care of me and my family during my husband's final illness.

Launie Gibson, the master stonemason who's work inspired this series.

About the Author

....

Best Selling author, Serena B. Miller, has won numerous awards, including the RITA and the CAROL. A movie, Love Finds You in Sugarcreek, was based on the first of her Love's Journey in Sugarcreek series, and won the coveted Templeton Epiphany award. Another movie based on her novel, An Uncommon Grace, recently aired on the Hallmark channel. She lives in southern Ohio in a house that her husband and three sons built. It has a wraparound porch where she writes most of her books. Her mixed-breed rescue dog, Bonnie, keeps her company while chasing deer out of the yard whenever the mood strikes. Her Manitoulin Island series is a labor of love based on many visits to the beautiful island.

www.serenabmiller.com

More books by
Serena B. Miller

LOVE'S JOURNEY ON MANITOULIN ISLAND SERIES:

Love's Journey on Manitoulin Island: Moriah's Lighthouse - Book I
Love's Journey on Manitoulin Island: Moriah's Fortress - Book II
Love's Journey on Manitoulin Island: Moriah's Stronghold - Book III

LOVE'S JOURNEY IN SUGARCREEK SERIES:

Love's Journey in Sugarcreek: The Sugar Haus Inn - Book I
    (Formerly : Love Finds You in Sugarcreek, Ohio)
Love's Journey in Sugarcreek: Rachel's Rescue - Book II
Love's Journey in Sugarcreek: Love Rekindled - Book III

THE UNCOMMON GRACE SERIES (AMISH):

An Uncommon Grace - Book I
Hidden Mercies - Book II
Fearless Hope - Book III

MICHIGAN NORTHWOODS SERIES (HISTORICAL):

The Measure of Katie Calloway - Book I
Under a Blackberry Moon - Book II
A Promise to Love - Book III

SUSPENSE:

A Way of Escape

COZY MYSTERY:

The Accidental Adventures of Doreen Sizemore

NON-FICTION:

More Than Happy: The Wisdom of Amish Parenting

VISIT **SERENABMILLER.COM** TO SIGN UP FOR
SERENA'S NEWSLETTER AND TO CONNECT WITH SERENA.

82258574R00117

Made in the USA
Columbia, SC
30 November 2017